THE FIR

The First Time

Broken Boys, Volume 1

Zane Menzy

Published by Zane Menzy, 2023.

This is a work of fiction. Similarities to real people, places, or events are entirely coincidental.

THE FIRST TIME

First edition. October 23, 2023.

Copyright © 2023 Zane Menzy.

ISBN: 979-8223545439

Written by Zane Menzy.

Michael S... Thank you for an unforgetabble summer of youth. It's a pity things went the way they did. But thanks for the lessons and the memories.

Chapter 1

I could tell Jockey was wasted the moment he opened the door. He stood there barefoot, wearing cheap satin boxers and a black singlet. A blue lava lamp bubbled away beside his bed, the dull light adding to the stoner atmosphere. Rap music was playing on his laptop.

"Dude! Get inside," he said. "You're letting the second-hand smoke out."

As soon as I entered the sleepout, he quickly closed the door behind me. We shook hands loosely and Jockey pulled me in for a bro-hug—the whiff of his pits telling me he could do with a shower.

Two years older than I was, Jockey was tall and skinny, standing about six-foot. Despite his height, people sometimes mistook us for being the same age. I think it was the baby face of his, those innocent brow eyes beneath inquisitive eyebrows, and his small ears sticking out beneath brown hair buzzed close to the scalp. Other things, mature details, gave away his real age of twenty; like the badly-drawn tattoos around his lanky arms and shoulders, and the hair on his lightly muscled chest and lean belly.

I stepped back and inhaled deeply, getting a hit of the pot smoke clogging the bedroom of his sleepout. It made a nice change from the usual stench of rancid socks and dirty undies that usually infested Jockey's living space. Although he earned enough money working as a labourer to afford to move out of home, he'd chosen to stay living with his aunt and uncle who'd raised him and his two older brothers. If you ignored the fact his uncle was a total cock, Jockey had a pretty good setup. The sleepout was more like his own one-bedroom apartment with its own private access onto the street. It also had a small kitchenette and bathroom which meant he rarely had to go inside the main house; unless he was raiding food from his aunt and uncle's pantry.

"How was work?" he asked lazily, playing with the pale little chin beard he had grown during the week. He hopped onto his bed and sat cross legged, and I spotted the sly droop of Jockey's uncut buddy.

"Work was quiet. Same as usual."

He eyed the shopping bag in my hand. "Did you bring the munchies?"

I passed him the snacks he'd asked me to pick up after I'd finished work. He wasted no time rifling through the selection of chips and candy I'd bought on the way over.

"Thanks, man." He pulled out a bag of Doritos and ripped into it. "With his mouth full, he asked, "Has Brian left for uni yet?"

"He left two days ago."

"You must be gutted. I know how much you'll miss them."

"I'm sure I'll survive," I said nonchalantly, playing down how much I was already missing my best friend. "He said he will be back for a visit at the end of the semester."

Jockey didn't respond, opting instead to hoover up another Dorito. While he was distracted with filling his face, I glanced over at the wall above the couch where a wonky-looking bookshelf he'd made housed a row of military books. I'm not sure if he'd ever read them or just had them there for show. The dude loved anything to do with war and explosions, whether it be in books, movies or video games. He would often talk about wanting to join the army or even the police force; any organisation that would supply him with a gun and a uniform. The problem was he was too lazy and unorganised to get off his ass and do anything about it. That was probably a good thing though. The thought of a reckless dipshit like Jockey wielding any sort of weapon was a terrifying prospect. Still, his love of the military came out in other ways like his book collection, his wardrobe filled with camo gear and his military-style haircut.

"You have good taste in chips, Michael," Jockey said, licking a finger covered in Dorito dust. "These are fucking tasty."

The reason for me picking the Doritos had less to do with taste and more to do with them being on special. When your only income came from working part-time in hospitality there wasn't much wriggle room to be fussy. Jockey was just lucky that I was willing to blow twenty bucks on junk food for him if it meant I got paid back in other ways. Ways that had me sneaking another glance at the pale droop of his dick resting against the dark hairs of his thighs.

"You can help yourself," he said, pointing to the bong beside his bed. "The bowl's packed."

I went over and fetched the bong and a lighter from the bedside table and sparked it up. *I wonder when he will start playing the porn?* I thought as I inhaled and held the smoke. Squinting into Jockey's boxers I saw that he was getting a chubby, hanging a little longer, a little fatter, taking a late afternoon stroll down to the ragged hem of his boxers.

Putting the Doritos down, Jockey uncrossed his legs, stretching them out, flexing his feet and cracking his toes. His growing erection was trapped and obvious under the silk boxers. He put a hand near it and gave me a look.

"You wanna bust a nut?" he asked.

I choked on the smoke.

"That's why you usually swing by here on Friday nights isn't it, dog?" Jockey said. "I mean, it ain't just the dope you come here for, is it?"

I shook my head, still unable to talk. I tried hard not to cough, but managed only to hack and wheeze like an old man. My eyes got teary and I couldn't catch my breath. I passed the bong back to Jockey, hacking away some more.

"You want some water?" he asked, one-eyed at the bong. He leaned back after his hit and smiled back at me.

I shook my head and finally got my coughing under control. Jockey hadn't been wrong about the reason behind my Friday night visits. Although we'd occasionally hang out on other days just to talk shit or play videogames, Friday nights were always about busting a nut. The way we usually got around to it was watching some porn on Jockey's laptop, rubbing our arousal through our clothes until Jockey would eventually sink to his knees and help me out. I liked it that way. It helped put distance between what I was doing and who I was doing it with.

He put the bong down and reached out for the hardened front of my jeans. I jumped back.

"Dude, don't tell me you're shy now," he said with a laugh. "I've been blowing you for nearly two years."

"Sorry. I'm just not used to you being so...forward."

"I wouldn't normally jump straight to it but I thought it might cheer you up with Brian leaving."

It would cheer me up, but that didn't mean I appreciated him talking about it openly. These suck sessions always happened naturally, quietly, secretly.

"So are you keen?" Jockey poked his togue against the inside of his cheek. "I can try swallowing you again if you want? But no promises I'll be able to keep it down. You do shoot pretty big loads."

Stop fucking talking about it!

Ignoring my annoyance with him for talking out loud about the one thing we never talked out loud about, I nodded and gave my consent.

He slid off the bed and walked towards me on his knees, coming to a stop right in front of me. I gulped back my nervous energy, the same feeling I always had when it was about to begin. Jockey's slender fingers made quick work of my zipper and he tugged down my jeans.

With my jeans around my ankles, and my cock sticking through the hole of my briefs, I let Jockey lick the tender tip. His fist covered most of the shaft, and the rest of it enjoyed the manipulations of Jockey's soft, wet lips. He slurped around the head, keeping a tight grip on the base, digging his tongue into the piss slit. I didn't know what to do with my hands, so I crossed them over my chest, blocking the view I had of Jockey's mouth working on me. I then moved my arms up over my head, but felt silly, like an aerobics instructor or something. Finally, I placed my hands on my hips, which made me feel like a posing pornstar getting his due.

"Suck it," I said silently, writing my own script, directing my own movie. "Suck that big dick."

As average as my dick was—six inches—whenever Jockey had his lips around my tool, I felt huge. Powerful. All mighty. I felt as if

I were invincible and understood, in that moment, man's desire to use another for his own personal pleasure.

Jockey shrugged out of this singlet. His skin was tanned, and he had the sinewy muscles of a skateboarder, no heaviness to him anywhere but his cock and balls. He had a surprising amount of hair down the front of him, particularly around his nipples and navel. He wasn't exactly my type, but I wasn't all too sure I had a type yet. I just enjoyed getting my dick sucked. Provided I closed my eyes then it could have been anyone down there.

Jockey played with my balls, stroking them, pulling them downward. I felt my nuts start to shrink up despite Jockey's tugging. I let myself moan a little, enjoying the noisy suck of Jockey's hard-at-work mouth, spit dropping down between us, and Jockey working his fingers back behind my balls and poking around my butthole.

"Not there," I growled. "Stay away from there."

"Sorry, bro." The words came out garbled around the head of my cock.

The horny fucker always tried to pull that move; slipping a digit in my backdoor. I may have been willing to let him suck my cock but there was no way I was letting *him* slip something in my backdoor, even if it was just a finger.

"Whoa," I said, opening my eyes and backing up.

Jockey looked up at me with his battered lips all wet. "What's wrong?"

"Just, um…" I stammered. "Just, go easy. I'm getting close."

"That's the whole fucking idea, dude," Jockey chuckled. "I'm trying to make you cum, remember?"

I knew that but I didn't want it to be over so quickly. Not before I'd had a chance to enjoy him licking my balls.

As if reading my mind, Jockey dipped lower and scooped my balls in his mouth, tonguing them delicately. I knew they'd be sweaty as fuck after a shift at work and then walking here, but he wasn't perturbed. He sucked down on the shaved orbs, absorbing my taste.

"Fuck yeah," I gasped. "You're so fucking good at that."

The words of praise urged him on and he slipped a hand inside his boxers and began to toss off. After a few strokes, he pulled the boxers down to release his cock and resumed his wank. I hated when he did that. Made me feel small. The scruffy redneck easily had an inch on me and a superior girth.

"Suck my cock again," I ordered. When he took my meat between his lips, I grabbed the back of his head and began fucking his mouth.

Jockey moaned, committing himself to a rough pounding.

Holding his head like a rugby ball I was on the verge of fumbling, I stuffed his mouth with my dick, making him choke and splutter. I think subconsciously this was my way of punishing him for pulling his dick out and making me feel small. If I couldn't beat him with inches then I'd beat him with the force of my helmet tickling his tonsils.

Like the trooper he was, Jockey took the rough onslaught, swallowing every cock-thrust while he jerked himself off below. Suddenly, I heard him make a squeak, like a high-pitched moan, and then I felt the reason why. He'd just lost his lollies all over the front of my legs. Warm rivulets of cum dribbled through the hair on my shins, snaking their way down to my ankles and socks.

I pushed him off my cock. I grabbed hold of my spit-soaked shaft and gave myself two tugs that unleashed a white flow of cum all over Jockey's nose, lips and bearded chin. While it would have been hot to see him swallow, I got just as powerful rush from spraying his face with my seed.

Rather than be offended by the facial I'd just given him, Jockey chuckled to himself as he used his discarded singlet to wipe his face. "Damn, son. You gave me quite the shower."

"Sorry," I lied.

"It's all good. As long as you had fun."

Jockey inspected the soiled singlet, smiling as he laid eyes on the sticky substance that until only moments ago had been swimming inside my balls. He then turned the singlet inside-out and used it to wipe up the mess he'd made on my legs. When he was done, he dragged himself up on his hands and knees before stumbling to his feet. He stood to face me, a friendly smile on his face as he watched me pull up my pants.

"Thanks, man," I mumbled. "I needed that."

"No worries, bro. You know I don't mind helping you out." He went and sat back down on his bed, rummaging through the bag of goodies I'd bought. "I reckon I just earned myself another bag of Doritos after that fine performance."

I always envied how calm Jockey was after the deed was done. Like it was no big deal. Meanwhile I'd be battling butterflies in my tummy and an avalanche of guilt. Right now was no exception as I stood there awkwardly watching him stuff his face.

"Am I right in thinking I'll be doing that more often?" he asked, munching on a chip. "Sucking your dick?"

"What makes you think that?"

"With Brian gone you'll probably be visiting me way more."

Staring around Jockey's messy shitpit of a room filled with its army memorabilia and drug paraphernalia, I couldn't help but feel a little depressed. A whispered and noncommittal "Maybe" was the best I could manage.

Chapter 2

TEN MINUTES LATER, I was out the door and on my way home. I never did stay long at Jockey's after I had emptied my balls, but this time I was especially keen to get out of there. I hadn't liked how he'd come out and asked if I wanted a blowie instead of just letting it happen, and how there'd been no porn on while we did it. I knew it was stupid but the porn acted like a shield, one I used to help deflect how queer the whole situation was.

Don't get me wrong, I was under no illusion I liked certain guys as much as girls but Jockey wasn't one of those certain guys. If I was going to explore my same-sex desire then it would have been with someone less Jockey and more stud. I know it made me an asshole but I was embarrassed to have a bro-job arrangement with a scruffy redneck with stinky pits and an aversion to washing his balls regularly. Everyone in town considered Jockey Savage a total dropkick. The only thing that made me okay with it was how the arrangement was purely a one-way street with my dick driving into his mouth.

And that we never talk about it!

Turning the corner at the end of Jockey's street, I headed in the direction of my house. It was a fifteen-minute walk if you were moving briskly, which was recommended in these parts after dark.

Jockey and I both lived in the Tamati subdivision with its cheap weatherboard homes and lack of shops and pretty parks. It had been built for the workers of a gas plant further up the valley constructed in the 1980s. Upon the gas plant's completion, the workers' abandoned houses became a beacon for the poor and unemployed. It wasn't a shanty town by any means, but compared to the average New Zealand suburb it was considered impoverished with every second house containing a tiny cabin in its yard to act as an extra bedroom for families coping with overcrowding.

Ten miles away, in what felt like a different world, Brian's family lived in the seaside village of Dusty Bay, home to the area's elite and retired farmers. You'd think this would have meant Jockey would be the one I hung out with the most because of the distance, but that wasn't the case. I would always take the bus or borrow Gavin's car to visit Brian over walking the short distance to Jockey's house. It wasn't until our 'Friday Fun' became a thing that I started visiting Jockey regularly, and like most mistakes it had come about by accident.

Brian had been away on holiday with his parents at the time, and I had found myself hanging out with Jockey instead. We'd been playing Xbox in his sleepout, talking shit, when at some point he told me he wanted to show me a porn clip he'd watched the night before.

"No thanks," I'd said, more interested in killing shit on the videogame.

"Trust me, bro. You'll like it. It's super hot."

"That's what you said last time and it turned out to be a chick shitting into a cup."

Jockey had laughed. "This time it's for real. You'll like it." Then he'd given me a condescending smile. "Unless you're scared of sex or some shit."

That had pissed me off so I'd put the controller down and told him to show me the video. I can't even remember what the video was of exactly, just some generic blond with some generic big-dicked dude. Anyway, it did the trick because within minutes I was sat there rubbing the growing mound in my jeans when I heard Jockey whisper, "Want some help?"

Too shocked to say no, too shocked to say anything, I'd let him help by rubbing me down there until I blew a wad in my undies. That's pretty much how it started. Overtime his 'help' grew from rubbing the outside of my jeans, to rubbing me inside my jeans, to then giving me handjobs, until finally one night my dick found its way inside his mouth, and every Friday night after that.

The only time I ever brought up our secret bro-job arrangement was after the first time he'd sucked me off. I mean, that was a big jump from lending a helping hand to a helping mouth.

"Are you queer?" I'd asked.

"Nar, bro. I like girls."

"Then why did you just suck my dick?"

He had shrugged and replied, "I just like to make you feel good. Besides, how else am I supposed to compete with Brian?"

I should have told him he didn't have to suck me off to compete with Brian, that we were mates regardless, but why give up a steady supply of blowjobs? I'm not a fucking moron. Selfish and horny yes, but not a moron.

So while it felt like I was fast becoming one of the oldest virgins in town, at least I'd been getting my dick sucked regularly since I was sixteen. A part of me wished I could have told Brian about how many times I'd been sucked off but I knew that wasn't a good idea. He would have told me to stop being a homo, although I'm sure if he were in my position then he would have quite happily let Jockey suck him off too.

But there were limits to Jockey's help. More than once during our sessions I'd tried to get him to bend over for me so I could try fucking him. It wasn't like I would explicitly say "Can I fuck you" but he usually got the jist of what I wanted when I'd try and push him towards the bed and turn him around. Each time I had tried this though, Jockey would laugh and shake his head. "Nar, bro." Then he'd just go back to sucking me off.

Fucker.

As I neared home, I pulled my phone out to see if I had any messages from Brian yet. Nope. I then checked his Instagram and saw he's uploaded two pictures; one of his dorm and the other of him sitting around with two guys in what looked like a communal lounge. Jealousy stabbed me in the gut. He'd only been gone 48 hours and already he'd found the time to make new friends but still hadn't sent me so much as a text message.

Meanwhile I'm stuck here with dipshit Jockey.

Jockey had always been my backup friend, the person I hung out with when Brian was too busy. And the truth was Brian had been busy a lot these past few months. But with Brian pissing off to university I'd probably have to elevate Jockey to best friend status. The thought was a depressing one. That's not to say I didn't like Jockey, but he was a bit of a social lepper. Sure, he could bring about laughter wherever he went, and he could be a lot of fun with the dumb shit he said and did, but the laughs were usually directed at him not with him.

I think part of the problem was his big personality, like a hyper kid in desperate need of Ritalin. Most people found him hard to handle. I know Brian always had, which is why Jockey had always been an afterthought to our friendship. More often than not, Jockey was purposely left out of our sleepovers or trips to the movies. In saying that, we had both been quick to make good use of our older friend when Jockey had turned eighteen, giving Jockey a list of alcohol to buy us for the weekends. But even this didn't stop Brian from badmouthing Jockey behind his back.

I think another reason for Brian's disdain was that he came from a good family and his parents did not approve of their son hanging around with trashy elements. Shit, they barely tolerated Brian's friendship with me, but Jockey...no way was that shit gonna fly. Jockey was a Savage—a surname often whispered with a judgmental tone in our town. Jockey had grown up the youngest of three boys and both older brothers were constantly in and out of prison. They weren't particularly dangerous the Savage brothers. non-violent, light-fingered opportunists, which perhaps made their reputation worse because they weren't exactly feared, just mocked.

Unfortunately for Jockey he was mocked most of all. He wasn't a thief like his brothers but he certainly had the most oddball personality of the bunch and it had ensured he'd remained unpopular from the moment he started school until the day he dropped out at sixteen.

Secretly, I enjoyed Jockey's big personality. He had no shame and never shied away from a dare. It didn't matter how dumb or crazy the dare was, he would always do it. He was also the most honest person I know. In fact, he was so honest that he was the only guy I knew growing up who'd openly admitted to tossing himself off, which wasn't something boys usually admitted to until they got a bit older. But not Jockey, he was openly talking about Mrs. Palmer and her five daughters by the time he was starting high school. It was because of his honesty I also knew he'd only ever slept with two women. The first was a hooker he'd paid for sex on the night of his eighteenth birthday, the other was a solo mum in her thirties who he'd dated for about ten months before she dumped him for being too immature and a bad role model for her three young children. It probably hadn't helped when she turned up to visit him at his sleepout and found a pair of her knickers hanging from a makeshift flagpole above his bed.

Interestingly, mine and Jockey's bro-job arrangement didn't stop during this time. It carried on like normal. Every Friday night. Sometimes I wondered if I should have felt guilty about that, or at least ask Jockey how he felt about it, but it had always been easier to label our arrangement as a form of mateship rather than something explicitly sexual.

Brian and I had given Jockey so much shit for dating an older woman with kids, teasing him by asking if her children were calling him daddy yet. Jockey took the piss-taking in his stride, usually just saying we were jealous that he was getting laid every night while we weren't. He hadn't been wrong. I'd been jealous as all hell. While no one could accuse his older girlfriend of being a supermodel, the blond Fiona was still quite a looker; pretty face, curvy in the right places and a pair of jugs that according to Jockey he'd jizzed over thirty-two times.

Yeah...he'd kept a tally. He was that sort of guy.

Suddenly, the feeling of Jockey's spit still stuck to my dick made me feel nauseous. I lowered a hand and manhandled my crotch, hoping my boxers might wipe away some of the damp residue. All that achieved was slathering his leftover drool around even more.

When I reached the gravel driveway to the 2-bedroom piece of shit I called home, I was relieved to see the lights weren't on. Gavin was either still at the pub or had gone to bed early. Getting pissed at the pub was the more likely scenario. He'd always enjoyed his booze, usually a few cold ones on the couch after a hard day's work at the local freezing works, but Gavin had become more sociable with his drinking after Mum ran off four years ago with a local musician called Ricky Rocker—clearly not the douchebag's real name—and moved to Australia.

Considering the level of Mum's betrayal—Ricky and Gavin had been good friends—I had half-expected Gavin to kick me out on my ass, but thankfully he didn't do that. He told me it wasn't my fault my mother was "a crazy bitch thinking with her cunt" and that I could stay as long as I wanted. His words about my mother were harsh, but not entirely inaccurate. The politest way to describe Joy Freeman would be that she was a free spirit who liked to have a good time—which might explain why the story of who my real father was had kept changing through the years.

She once told me that my dad was an Australian soldier, on leave, who took her to the cinema on her night off from working as a barmaid. He promised to come back and marry her, she said, when his next tour of duty was complete. Another time, when she was pissed on gin, the story went that my dad was a handsome fortune teller who she had met at a gypsy fair. Then he was a professional kickboxer competing in a national tournament.

The reality was she didn't have a clue who my father was. He could have been any one of a dozen horny bastards who had fucked her the summer I was conceived. Considering my mother was an exotic beauty with her dark hair and Māori ancestry, the only real guess I could make about my father was he must have been hardcore Caucasian for me to wind up a pasty pale whitetail with dirty-blond hair and green eyes.

When I was eight, Mum eventually curbed her sluttish ways when she settled down with Gavin. Ten years younger than my mother, Gavin had been besotted with her the first time she served him a drink in the pub, insisting he'd never seen a woman more beautiful. Maybe Mum's ego was wooed by the compliments, or maybe she just had a thing for younger men who could match her own high sex drive. Whatever the reason, Gavin and Mum stuck together for nearly a decade until she'd run off.

As far as stepfathers went—and I suppose that's what he was even though the pair never married—Gavin was chill as fuck. Provided I paid my board each week he let me do what I want.

As I unlocked the door and stepped inside, I could tell by the absence of snoring Gavin must have been out. I made a beeline to the bathroom. I needed a shower so I could wash Jockey's spit off my cock. I also suspected he'd missed some spots when wiping up the mess, traces of his semen now drying to the hairs on my legs.

Slipping off the jeans and T-shirt I wore, I messed with hot and cold until I got the shower warm enough to step into. Through the glass enclosure, I could just barely see my reflection in the mirror over the sink. I patted my tummy, wishing the flat surface had a clearer outline of abs. Even so, what I saw staring back at me didn't look too bad: five-ten, slim and toned with shoulder-length dark blond hair. Gavin would often lecture me about my hair, constantly telling me I'd look better with it cut short. The man was dreaming. There were no short back and sides in my future. It had been this length since I was fourteen, a visual representation of my childhood dream to become a rock star like Kurt Cobain. Sadly I didn't have an ounce of musical talent in my body so I'd settled instead just for the long hair and a wardrobe consisting of black t-shirts, ripped jeans and skuddy sneakers.

When I got out of the shower, I saw that I'd missed a call from Brian. He hadn't forgotten about me! With the excitement of a child on Christmas morning, I dialed my voicemail, keen to hear what Brian had to say. All I could hear was the sound of music blaring over the top of muffled voices. After about twenty seconds of this I finally heard Brian's gravelly voice say to someone "Oh fuck. I just butt-dialled someone." There was laughter from what sounded like two other guys and then the call abruptly ended.

Chapter 3

I KNEW IT WAS A DREAM when Brian walked into my bedroom wearing nothing but a smile and a hard-on. But that didn't stop me from taking advantage of the situation, or him for that matter. Somehow I knew I wouldn't have long before I'd be waking up, virginal and horny, so time was of the essence here. Dragging my best mate to the bed, I forced him to turn around and started fucking his pale ass immediately, making sure he felt every dreamy inch.

"You like it rough, don't you, Brian?"
"Yeah."
"You miss me don't you, Brian?"
"Yeah."
"And you love me, don't you Brian?"
"Yeah."
"And you want me to—"
"Piss in my ass!" Brian looked over his shoulder at me and smiled dementedly. *"Do it, Mike. Fill me with your piss. As much as you like."*
"Don't be so dirty, Brian."
"Just do it, Mike. Piss in me. Piss in me. Piss in me. Piss in me..."

And that's when Brian and the dream faded to nothing and I woke up realising my bladder was full. Turned out that dream Brian wasn't just a kinky sicko; he was also a piss psychic. While I was grateful to have not pissed the bed, I would have still liked to have at least had a wet dream first. Unlike Brian—the real one, not the kinky dream slut version—who'd once confided in me how he'd wake up most mornings with cummy pyjama pants, I'd never actually had that many wet dreams. Three maybe? Probably because I wanked too much was my best guess. I don't think a single day had gone by without me tossing off since I'd discovered the joys of masturbation at thirteen. I could have been crippled in bed with Covid and I'd still find the strength to rub one out.

I lay still for a moment, listening to my surroundings through the thin walls of my bedroom. In the kitchen, Gavin was already making breakfast. I could hear the scrape of a knife, which meant he was buttering his charred toast. In the bathroom, I could hear someone taking a shower and singing. It sounded like a woman.

Sounds like somebody got lucky last night.

I wasn't thrilled because I needed to use the toilet, which of course was in the bathroom currently occupied by Gavin's hookup. My bladder wasn't about to wait for the warbling Beyonce wannabe in there to finish her shower, so I ambled over to the bedroom window, opened it, and showered the weeds below with a lengthy piss. With that morning chore out of the way, I took care of the second and equally important task at hand; finishing off what the dream had started—which I managed to do in less time than it had taken me to piss out the window.

High on the relief of empty balls and an empty bladder, I decided to go chat with Gavin in the kitchen and hopefully get a look at this mystery woman he'd brought home. I slipped into my clothes from the night before—jeans and a black T-shirt crumpled on the floor—then padded barefoot into the kitchen where I found a groggy-looking Gavin sat at the table with two plates of toast.

"Are one of those for me?" I joked, pretending to grab one.

"Not unless you're the one who gave me head before bed, then no."

"TMI, dude! TMI!" I sniggered as I made my way towards the kettle. "So who is she?"

"Ask her yourself when she gets out."

"Okay."

"Seriously. Can you ask her?"

Turning back to Gavin, I saw a genuine worry on his face as he raked a hand through his wavy black hair. "Oh my God." I began smirking. "You can't remember her name, can you?"

"Keep your bloody voice down," he hissed, gaze aimed in the direction of the bathroom. "I was drunk as a skunk last night. I can't even remember how we got back here."

"But you can remember the blowjob?"

"Obviously my dick has a better memory than I do." He cast a playful glance down at his crotch and smiled. "And apparently he's quite the soldier to have battled his way through brewer's droop."

With a snort, I continued with my mock repulsion. "Could you wait until I've had something to eat before you start talking about your cock. I'd rather have something in my stomach before I throw up."

"You might think I'm vomit-inducing but I'll have you know that the ladies at the pub think otherwise. One of them told me I look like a younger Taika Waititi."

Raising a sardonic brow. "Is that a compliment though?"

"Cheeky shit." Gavin laughed. "And of course it's a bloody compliment. That man's a national treasure *and* he used to play a stripper on tv."

"Well, clearly we know what your next career move should be then."

Lifting his t-shirt, Gavin winked at me as he gave his hairy tummy a pat. "I've certainly got the body for it."

In his mid-thirties, Gavin had the body of a man who had probably once been a high school athlete, but who had gone slightly soft thanks to too many beers and too many hours in front of the television watching rugby games he dreamed about playing in himself. However, compared to the average punter pissing it up at the local tavern he was probably considered a bit of alright by the few women who went there.

When we heard the bathroom door open, Gavin whispered, "Ask her what her name is."

I quickly poured myself a hot drink and went and sat down at the kitchen table with Gavin. As we waited for his mystery lay to appear in the kitchen, I toyed with the idea of asking Gavin to introduce us. While it would have been hilarious to watch the man squirm, I didn't want to embarrass his one-night-stand by doing that. But as it turned out I didn't have to ask for her name. I already knew her.

"Fiona?" I half-blurted.

Still drying her blond hair with a towel, Fiona cast me a confused smile. "Yes?" She didn't remember me.

"You two know each other?" Gavin asked.

Fiona tilted her head, studying me for a moment. "Oh...of course. You're one of Matthew's friends, aren't you?"

"Yeah," I said, finding it weird to hear someone call Jockey by his real name.

"How is he?"

"He's good."

"Who's Matthew? Gavin asked.

"Jockey," I said. "Matthew's his real name."

"Really?" Gavin still looked confused. "I never knew Jockey wasn't his real name."

I cast my stepfather a *are-you-for-real?* face. "You actually thought his parents called their kid Jockey?"

"I just figured they were fans of horse racing."

I would have laughed but I was still too shocked that Gavin had spent the night with Jockey's ex missus. This was the sort of thing that if Bian were around I'd have called him and told him about. He would have found it fucking hilarious, which it sort of was.

"So how do you know Jockey?" Gavin asked Fiona.

"I got to know Matthew when he and his uncle renovated the unit I was renting last year." She took a sip on her coffee. "Lovely guy but very immature."

I sat there waiting for her to say he was her ex but she didn't. And judging by the discreet *don't-say-a-fucking-word* look she flicked my way, she didn't want me to bring it up either.

"I still can't believe I never knew the lad's real name." Gavin turned to me and asked, "So why do youse call him Jockey?"

"Because he was a short little runt as a kid."

"He was, wasn't he?" Gavin said, more to himself than anyone else. "A real pip squeak of a boy."

"So what are your plans for today?" Fiona asked Gavin.

As if it were happening in slow motion, Gavin's gaze hovered over Fiona's tits then up to her face, and back down to her tits, then finally back to her face. I could tell he was sizing her up in his now sober state. Then came the flirt: "I was thinking I might take a certain beautiful lady out for lunch...if she cares to join me that is?"

I resisted the urge to roll my eyes as I watched him reach out and stroke her arm. The guy was all cheese, but it was smooth cheese.

Fiona giggled like a girl half her age. "Lunch sounds lovely."

Out of loyalty to Jockey, I threw out a comment I knew would throw a cat amongst the pigeons. "But what about Betsy?" I looked at Gavin. "I thought you had a date with her today?"

Fiona's face soured. "Who is Betsy? You told me last night that you were single."

Gavin glared in my direction. "Ignore the resident shit-stirrer over there. Betsy is the name of my bus."

"I think the technical term is paperweight on wheels," I chimed in.

"Don't talk about the old girl like that. She's part of the family," Gavin said, only half-joking.

I actually felt sort of guilty for what I'd said. I too was quite attached to Betsy. She'd doubled as a playhouse for me as a child before Gavin started doing her up to try and create his ideal motorhome. As a child I'd entertained myself with visions of all the cool places we would drive Betsy to go see. Mum and I had never been to the South Island but Gavin had promised a ten-year-old me that when he got Betsy going again, we would all go as a family to explore Queenstown and Fiordland, and he would show us around his hometown of Invercargill right at the bottom of the South Island.

While many povo households like ours had dead vehicles in their yards, the difference here was that Gavin loved the rusted hunk of metal as if Betsy were a living creature. Despite the fact she was rusted to buggery and had no motor, Gavin had spent years on slowly converting her into his dream motorhome. He'd stripped out all the seats, installed two beds, kitchen and a coffin-like shower. A new motor and the rust work that needed doing still looked years off though, like never-gonna-happen years off. He had managed to save a lot of money on Betsy by going *treasure hunting*. That's what he called his trips to the dump to find anything he could use for Betsy's makeover. I'd gone with him all the time as a kid, excited to be helping make our dream holiday come true, but I'd stopped going with him when I turned thirteen after Brian told me I didn't want to get a reputation.

Fiona glanced dozily out the window and locked eyes on the monstrosity clogging our backyard. "It's so cute how you gave her a name."

Gavin sat back in his chair, nodding thoughtfully. "Yes, every queen deserves a name."

"Something you and Ru Paul both agree on," I said.

"Haven't you got something better to do, Mikey." He glared across the table at me. "Like washing your balls with a cactus leaf."

Sniggering, I left them to it and escaped to my bedroom. I was glad to be out of the kitchen. The last thing I wanted on a Saturday morning was to watch the mating rituals of the over thirty.

Sitting on my bed, I contemplated what to do with what looked like another perfectly sunny day. I didn't have a shift at the cafe until Tuesday which meant three days of freedom. As I thought about how empty my social calendar was now with Brian gone, I began to wonder if it was time to pick up some extra shifts.

Gavin had suggested I put my name down for a job at the freezing works. He said he'd put in a good word for me. But I didn't want to work with meat carcasses or stand on a production line anymore that I wanted to serve snoot locals flat whites and salads. The truth was I didn't know what I wanted to do, other than I wished I could buy a bus ticket and haul my ass out of my nowhere town.

I was well aware that the textbook path to leaving one's shitty hometown was to do what Brian was in the process of doing: move away and study, get a degree, graduate and get a high-paying job in an even bigger city so you can then gloat via Instagram with pictures showing the losers back in your hometown how happy and accomplished you were.

But there was just one problem with that—I was the loser who would be waiting for others envious pics to be posted to Instagram. Shit, I was already jealous based on the two pics Brian had uploaded. And I knew it would only get worse as the months and years wore on.

I was smart enough to get into uni, my grades proved it, but I was also smart enough to know the cost of study outweighed the benefit for someone in my situation. Besides, the only shit that interested me study-wise were subjects ending in ology; psychology, sociology, anthropology, criminology. And let's be honest, Professor YouTube could teach me most of that shit for free without lumbering me with a debt I'd spend years paying back.

So while I'd known for years I would not be escaping Moa Hill the way most young people did, I was still trying to come up with a plan that would deliver my ass somewhere with brighter lights. My current dream was to get published and become a famous author. I'd already written two books, both of them mystery novels, but so far they remained in a folder on my laptop unread. Well, aside from the handful of agents I'd submitted them to and had no response from.

I'd always been a book lover, horrors, thrillers and mysteries mostly, and began writing my own stories after Mum had runaway. It was the perfect escape and allowed me to get lost in the characters' lives I created. I'd decided that if I couldn't have control over what happened in the real world then at least I could exert some authority in a fictional one. Unlike my childish rockstar dreams that were hounded by the absence of any musical talent, I did discover that I at least had some ability with writing. Some of the lines were a bit choppy, and commas were still my number one enemy, but I knew instinctively the stories themselves were good. Or at least that's what I kept telling myself. While it seemed unlikely I would ever get the chance to see one of my stories in a bookshop, I still held out hope that something good would come from these stories that had come about from a very dark time in my life.

Gavin was a fucking legend the way he had fussed over me those first few months after Mum had left, neglecting his own emotions to worry about mine. I tried not to let him though, knowing he must have been hurting as well. I always downplayed her absence, saying I didn't miss her. These days I genuinely didn't miss Mum that much at all, but that hadn't been the case for the first two years. While it was true Joy Freeman had never been the poster girl for stability, she had at least been around, and in my fourteen-year-old brain at the time she was an essential part of our three-person family. So when she up and disappeared one day, only letting us know she was alright four days later via a postcard from Australia, and after Gavin had filed a missing person's report, I had been left numb. Her betrayal had made me less trusting, and more appreciative of loyalty.

Which is why you're a fucking asshole Brian Quayle! Just text me already.

And right at that moment, my phone chirped three times in quick succession, indicating a text message. Thinking my prayers had been answered, I excitedly swiped the screen only to be met with disappointment. "Oh," I said coolly when I saw Jockey's name instead of Brian's.

Jockey: Wanna hang this afternoon? I can come to yours if you like?

My mind began playing a reel of Jockey walking in and freaking out when he saw Fiona and Gavin together. Maybe it was just my imagination assuming he would freak out. But the thing was I didn't know how he'd react so I quickly fired back a text and told him I'd come visit him instead.

I searched my room for a clean pair of socks and failed to find any. I ended up settling on the two that smelled least bad—one blue, one white—then chucked on a pair of worn canvas sneakers. As I passed by the kitchen, I saw Gavin and Fiona necking like horny teenagers. I didn't bother telling Gavin I was going out, leaving him to make out with a woman who I hoped would remain a one-night stand. Anybody stupid enough to hook up with an idiot like Jockey Savage was best to be avoided.

It took me a moment to realise that I'd just insulted myself.

Chapter 4

MY WALK TO JOCKEY'S was interrupted by Damian Takarangi. A local man who had fallen on tough times and could often be found sleeping rough with his backpack of possessions. I'm sure he received a benefit of some sort but it was safe to say nearly every dollar of it went on drugs.

Closer to thirty than twenty, and closer to skinny that muscular, the once well-built Māori man looked meaner than what he actually was. His untamed facial hair, always seeming to hover somewhere between a beard and scraggly stubble, didn't help. He also didn't do himself any favours by walking around most days in a dark leather jacket covered in patches of rugby league club logos. I suppose it was the only one he owned but the bloody thing had earned him more than one hiding in the past from out-of-town thugs passing through the neighbourhood and mistaking him as a rival gang member.

A decade ago, Damian Takarangi had been a gym-obsessed nineteen-year-old whose passions were pretty girls and rugby league. He had worked part time as a bouncer at the same tavern my mum had worked as a barmaid. He'd even babysat me a couple times, thrilling me with ghost stories that would have me seeping with the light on. Unfortunately Damian wound up discovering the joys of synthetic cannabis and took such a liking to it that he ended up losing his job, his fitness, his girlfriend, contact with his two kids. The only thing he'd gained since then was a couple stints in prison for burglary.

To many in the neighbourhood, Damian Takarangi was a variation of the cliché "an accident looking for a place to happen": the former bouncer was a victim looking for a place to destroy himself.

Judging by the vacant look in his eyes, I figured he was off his face right now. That suspicion was confirmed when he approached me and started giving me his usual spiel to try and get money from strangers. "Hey, man. Sorry to bother you but could I trouble you for a couple dollars? My car broke down and my girlfriend and the kids are in the car. We're just trying to get enough so we can take my daughter who's sick to the hospital."

Now, if you did not know Damian the way to make him leave was to offer to go with him to the petrol station and fill the can yourself. But because I did know Mr high-as-a-fucking-kite, I just said, "Damian, it's me. Mike. Michael Freeman?"

He squinted at me.

"You used to work with my Mum at the River Tavern. Joy Freeman?"

"Oh, chur bro. Mikey Mike. How are you?" He proceeded to give me a handshake, the sort where I had no fucking idea where my thumb or fingers were supposed to go. "How's your mum? I haven't seen her around in ages."

"She's living in Australia, remember?"

"Oh yeah… with that singer guy. Ricky Rude, is it?"

"Rocker," I begrudgingly corrected. Although in our house he was known as Rick the prick.

He started smiling, like he was remembering better times, suddenly coming across like the Damian I remembered from years gone by. "Your mum was always a hard case, bro. Pretty too. *Real* pretty." He chuckled mischievously, probably about a memory I didn't care to know about. "How's your dad doing?"

I didn't bother correcting that mistake. "Gavin's good."

Just as quickly as the clarity had come back to him, it left just as abruptly as he started eyeing up my pockets. "You got a spare smoke, bro? I'm hanging out for one, aye."

"I don't smoke." *Unless I'm drinking.*

"Bugger." He looked at my pockets again. "Got ten bucks you could spare?"

"No sorry." I could smell that he needed a shower, badly, so I asked, "Have you got a place to stay at the moment?"

"Yeah. I'm staying in one of the cabins at the campground."

"Do they have a shower block? Cos if they don't Gavin won't mind if you want to come round and use ours."

I was worried he might find the offer rude but he appeared to give it some serious thought until he got distracted by a woman across the road pushing a baby in a pram. Without any goodbye, he crossed the street to the young mother and delivered her his usual spiel, "Excuse me, miss, sorry to bother you but my car's broken down and..."

I continued on my way to Jockey's house, wondering if Damian would find someone stupid enough to give him some money. As I turned the corner onto Jockey's street, I could hear the noise of a saw roaring through the neighbourhood. This meant one thing: my army-obsessed buddy was inside his uncle's shed working on whatever his latest project was. Jockey fancied himself a bit of a handyman, but I think he just enjoyed working with sharp objects.

The idiot nearly lost a finger when he'd made the bookcase in his room.

Rather than take the shortcut to his sleepout via the side fence, I made my way down the driveway of Jockey's family home, avoiding being seen by his uncle who I could see slugging back a beer in the lounge. While each of the Savage boys stood about six foot, their uncle Chris was even taller, standing about six-foot-four, earning him the nickname Stretch.

The story behind why Jockey and his siblings were raised by his father's baby brother and his wife Jocelyn was a sad one. Jockey's parents had been driving home drunk from a party and crashed head-on with a milk tanker, leaving them as mangled as the hunk of metal they'd been travelling in. Instead of being pawned off to their grandparents, the Savage boys, aged two, four and six at the time, were given to their aunt and uncle after Jocelyn had discovered she could not have children. She'd raised them as if they were her own kids, but Jockey's uncle had never seemed too keen on playing dad to kids that weren't his own.

At the end of the driveway, I went through the small gate leading into the backyard. To the left was Jockey's sleepout, to the right was the jungle-like lawn dotted with neglected fruit trees. Walking through the long grass of the Savage's backyard, I couldn't help but chuckle knowing Jockey's aunty had probably been yelling at her deadbeat husband to mow the lawns. I'd heard Jocelyn scream at the top of her lungs numerous times telling her unemployed husband to, "Get off ya lazy ass and mow those fucking lawns, Chris."

A wrinkled bag of bones who could gain employment as a screaming banshee, Jocelyn Savage was the opposite of my soft-spoken pretty mother in more ways than one. Aside from a tough life beating her with the fugly stick and ageing her prematurely, Mrs Savage often came across like a grouchy bitch who never seemed in a good mood. The other difference was that although my mum came across sunny and nice, Jockey's aunt actually gave a shit about the three boys she'd raised as her own. She didn't forget their birthdays and she sure as shit wouldn't run off and leave them when they were just fourteen. To be honest, I'd been jealous of Jockey sometimes, wishing my mum was more like Jocelyn.

But my jealousy did not include Mr Savage. No siree. Give me Gavin any day of the week. Jockey's uncle was a royal prick who thought his shit didn't stink, despite the fact he was a jobless knuckle-dragger whose main skill was belching beer-scented burps. Worse than that though was the filthy temper on him when he got too drunk, which I gathered was a lot. Growing up Jockey used to come to school with bruises on his legs and back. He would tell teachers that he'd fallen out of a tree, again. It was when I was twelve and he was fourteen that he confided in me the truth about why he'd been away from school for two days before returning with two black eyes. His uncle had got drunk and beat him. I remember pleading with him to tell someone about the abuse, a teacher maybe, but Jockey insisted he was fine and that families didn't rat on each other. Thankfully Jockey's growth spurt at fifteen saw an end to his beatings when his uncle must have realised that his nephew could match him in a fight, maybe even win.

It was because of all that I couldn't understand why Jockey still lived at home. His older brothers had both fucked off as soon as they could, leaving him the only one still in the nest. It wasn't like he didn't earn enough money to get his own place. It didn't have to be flash, just somewhere away from his piss-head uncle, because even though Mr Savage may have stopped hitting Jockey all those years ago, I suspected living with him was still no picnic.

When I rounded the last fruit tree in my way, I found a shirtless Jockey working on the concrete pavement outside the front of shed. He had his back to me, hunched over a large sheet of wood resting on two saw-horses. He must had been working in the sun for a while because his tanned back was dripping beads of sweat, wetting the waistband of the orange boardshorts he had on. From this angle he looked almost malnourished, but his slenderness was deceptive. There was a sinewy strength to him, a clench of muscle around his shoulder blades and along the furrow of his spine. I'd seen him get in a couple scraps at school and bullies soon learned to not underestimate him.

While he sawed through the wood, I took the opportunity to study the vine-like tattoos on his shoulders and biceps. I think they were supposed to be some sort of Māori koru design, but Jockey's brother Darren—who'd done them—couldn't draw for shit and they looked more like weeds in my opinion. Still, I know Jockey liked them so I'd kept that opinion to myself. The other thing I had always kept to myself was how I secretly desired the next part of Jockey's body I checked out—his ass.

A small, neat ass, topping slim thighs, it was most definitely Jockey's best feature, and such a pity it was attached to him. Having seen it during our Friday night sessions, I knew it looked even better naked, and was the reason why I'd attempted—and failed—to bend him over more than once. I pictured myself ramming him from behind, forcing him to bend over the sawhorse; his mouth stretched in a panting snarl of orgasm. Warm semen seeping from a deeply fucked hole.

I fucking felt like a perv, the crotch of my jeans stretched tight, my cock heavy with this awkward interest in my trashy mate's ass. I quickly shooed the image away, not wanting to greet him with a boner. Rather than sneak up on him and risking him cutting off a finger, I hung back and waited for him to turn around on his own accord.

When he finally did turn around and saw me, he smiled like I'd just made his day. He put the electric saw to the side and removed his ear muffs. "You came!"

"I said I would."

He packed away what he'd been working on, a chair apparently, and we then made our way to his sleepout to hang out. I'd only seen him last night so didn't have much to talk about, but that didn't stop Jockey telling me about how he'd spent the morning spying on Mrs Bedford, a middle-aged housewife who lived next door and liked to sunbathe topless. He'd been doing this for years, spying on her from what he called his 'wanking window' located at the rear of the sleepout.

"You have got to stop spying on your neighbour," I said with a chuckle. "You know you'll get in shit if she catches you. Her husband's built like a brick shithouse. And he used to be a boxer."

"I could take the old prick down." Jockey lifted an arm and tensed his bicep, sending an unwanted waft of his fresh sweat my way. "I've been working out. See."

"I'd still put money on the former boxer to win that fight. No offense."

"Pfft. Ye of little faith."

"Anyway, I'm sure Mrs Bedford wouldn't be too thrilled to know you've been perving at her old titties."

"Nar, bro. She fucking loves it. A woman her age is desperate for a young man in his prime to nut off over her."

"Or nut into the Fleshlight you keep under your bed, you mean."

"If you must know, it's stored in the utility room with the rest of my goodies."

The utility room was a windowless cave that you accessed from the bathroom. I'd only been in there once. Jockey kept it locked. It was L-shaped and was more like an overgrown wardrobe filled with shelves where Jockey stored his old toys, army memorabilia, and his Fleshlight apparently. I had always suspected he had other kinky items stored in there he didn't want others to see. I based that solely on his stories about Fiona and how he claimed she was into BDSM: rope play, whips, chains and shit like that. Considering how desperate Jockey had been to please his ex-girlfriend when they first got together it was safe to assume he would have invested in such items.

"If you're jealous you can join me. I'm ordering a new Fleshlight soon so you can use my old one. There's enough room at the window for both us."

The worst part about that sentence wasn't just how gross it was, it was that Jockey's offer was a serious one.

"That's a hard pass," I said. "I don't wanna put my dick in something you spunk into."

"You don't seem to have any problem putting your dick in my mouth."

His words were so unexpected I nearly fell off the chair. "Uh…"

"Bro, why are you so weird when I bring that up?"

"I just don't like talking about it." I bristled like an old prude. "I don't like how gay it is."

"There's nothing gay about a mate helping another mate out. That's all it is."

"Maybe," I replied, not entirely believing that. "But why are you bringing it up all of a sudden. We've never really talked about it before."

"I just figured that with Brian moving away you and me could just be a little bit more open about it. It doesn't have to be a big deal. Shit, we could do it more often if you were down for that."

"You want to suck my dick more often?"

He laughed. "Now it definitely sounds gay when you put it like that. What I mean is, I would like to make you *feel good* more often. I like to see my friends happy. And I know how happy you are when you stick your dick in my—"

"I get it," I said swiftly. "It makes me feel good."

"Have you ever wondered what would happen if you just, like, fucking unbottled yourself for five minutes? Just let go and did whatever the fuck you want?"

I felt an overwhelming sense of shame for both my gutlessness and my arrogance. Gutless because I had never told him, or anyone for that matter, about my bisexuality. And arrogant because even if I did tell him I was into guys, he wasn't one of them—unless he was willing to bend over and take it from behind so I didn't have to know it was Jockey Savage I was bumming.

Jockey mistook my guilt for more discomfort and backed off like he usually did. While I felt bad about it, I also felt good knowing I was the more dominant male. There was a thrill in that. The truth was I didn't feel like much of an alpha in other circles but when I was alone with Jockey I felt like the boss.

Thankfully Jockey's wafer-thin attention span meant we were already onto a new topic as he began to tell me how he'd approached a local scout group and asked if they needed help with leading any of the troops. In a way it was sort of sweet to think my knucklehead buddy wanted to help the community, but I also understood why the scout master had politely declined Jockey's offer.

"I can't believe they turned me down. I thought they were crying out for male role models for boys. Masculinity being in crisis and all that bullshit. Well, hello? What do you call me? A masculine role model."

"Or a stoner who jerks off while spying on his unsuspecting neighbour?"

"I bet old Dave the scout master does the exact same shit." Jockey went on, and on, and on, as he berated this Dave person and continued to crow about his merit as a male role model.

There was no point in responding.

"Whakarongo mai," Jockey said, pointing to his ears.

"I am listening to you."

"Well, don't you think it's bullshit? Them not letting me be a scout leader?"

"Did you stop to think they said no because you were never in the scouts yourself?"

"Should it matter? I know plenty of shit about surviving in the wilderness, like how to kill shit and tie knots. I tied Melissa to the bed enough times to learn a thing or two about rope."

"That there's your problem."

"What?"

"No offense but putting you in charge of a group of young kids would be like including cancer in a list of agreed ingredients for school lunches."

He blinked at me. "I ain't gonna fuck them."

Trying not to laugh, I replied, "I never said you were gonna fuck them, weirdo. But you will corrupt them in other ways."

"Like what?"

"Like telling them certain stories you shouldn't."

He shrugged and changed the topic once again. "So what are you getting me for my birthday? It's only a week away."

"The same thing I get you every year. A tinny."

"You could spruce it up a bit considering it's my twenty-first."

"I would but I don't have that much money."

"Lucky for you then that I know something you could get me that is free."

"What's that?"

"Well...I bought myself an early birthday present online and I was wondering if you'd be my guinea pig and let me use it on you."

"If you're talking about that taser you've been wanting you can forget it. That shit would hurt like a bitch."

"It's not the taser. Although that would be fun to use on you." He waggled his eyebrows. "I've ordered a milking machine."

"A what?"

"Let me show you what I'm talking about." He leapt to his feet and raced over to grab his laptop then returned to sit beside me, fingers tapping furiously at the keyboard. "It's this," he said, pointing at a machine that looked foreign to me. "You put that tube over your cock, it's hooked up to the machine, and it basically drains all the cum out of your balls. I've been wanting one for years. Fiona had a friend who owned one. Their cool as."

"And you want to use it." I stared at him blankly. "On me?"

"Yeah. It'd be fun. The chair you saw me working on is to go with it. You sit down, let yourself get strapped in, then let me put it on your knob and Bob's your uncle."

"Bob can fuck off. I'm not letting you tie me up and put a machine on my dick."

"It's totally safe."

"So is bungy jumping but I ain't hurling myself off a fucking bridge."

"Aw, but it's my birthday. You know birthday dares are part of our tradition."

Jockey was only partially right. The birthday dare bullshit was something he and Brian did mostly, but of course I'd occasionally be dragged into it by default. For the most part it was harmless fun, the sort of shit idiot mates did together. The funniest one was Brian's sixteenth birthday when he'd dared Jockey to go into Bed, Bath & Beyond and sing LMFAO's *I'm Sexy And I Know It* to the girl behind the counter, while doing the tragic dance moves. Security was called and Jockey earned himself a two-year ban from the store. He didn't seem bothered, but then he wasn't the sort of guy to buy pretty soaps.

"I think this might be asking a bit much to use it on the birthday dare ritual," I said, avoiding eye contact. "Just use it on yourself. That's clearly why you bought it. You don't need me to be the guinea pig."

"But I wanna hear the noises you make."

"What noises?"

"When we do that *thing* we do that you don't like me talking about, one of my favourite things is the noises you make. Their cute. And this will make you make a lot of those noises."

To be told my orgasmic moans were 'cute' felt a bit rude. I'd have rather been told they were sexy, or manly, but cute?

"So that's what I want for my birthday," Jockey said. "A tinny and two hours of you sat in the chair while I play with the dial."

"Two hours? You're fucking dreaming."

"It's the birthday dare, Mike. You know it's sacred. A man should always keep his word."

"I haven't even given you my fucking word."

"But you have to. It's a birthday dare."

"It's not exactly a normal dare, though, is it? You're asking me to take part in some sort of kink."

He shrugged. "What's a bit of kink between friends?"

Rather than get stuck debating a subject I'd rather avoid, I just told him, "I'll think about it."

"You're the man. Thank you." He gave me a hug. "Luff ya."

"Settle down. I only said I'll *think* about it." Pushing his arms away from me, I pointed to the price on the screen. "How can you afford this thing anyway? That's over two grand."

"It's called Easy Pay. I've been paying it off the past eight weeks."

"You're insane. You do realise you would get the same thrill for free with your hand, right?"

"I guess we will find out on my birthday. When Mikey's balls are strapped in for a night of bliss." He started to laugh as he made a jokey grope at my nuts.

Jockey may have been laughing but *Mikey's balls* were shrivelling to the size of peas.

Chapter 5

MY JOB AT CHAOS DIDN'T pay much above minimum wage, but it was enough to keep me clothed, fed, and anesthetized on the weekends. I hated doing closing shifts though. For starters it was always dead straight after six pm when the small space would transform from café to bar mode. The lack of customers made my five-hour shift drag out and feel like ten. Adding to the misery of the closing shift was I'd usually have to work with fuckface Chad who just so happened to be the son of the owner.

Chad was a hipster dude in his mid-twenties with the de rigueur scraggly goatee, sleeve tats and sock cap, working here at Chaos when he wasn't in art school classes. Hairy and fleshy—more fit-fat than chunky—he was surprisingly popular with girls despite not being the most handsome dude on earth. I guess it helped that he was tall. Tall and confident. Tall, confident and rich. Tall, confident, rich and an asshole.

As a regular-sized, povo introvert who tried his best not to be an asshole, I knew too well how most girls loved guys like Chad. All the girls who worked here certainly did. He'd hooked up with enough of them. I think that's why his mum Carol had started making us work the closing shift together. She probably hoped my lack of tits would be less distracting.

But it didn't stop Chad from helping himself to the alcohol behind the bar as soon as the only customers we'd had all night got up to leave.

While I went to wipe down the table, Chad gulped down the RTD Smirnoff he'd helped himself from the fridge. I could sense he wanted to talk. Of the male staff members who worked here, it was me he gravitated towards the most. I couldn't be sure why but my guess was that because I wore my hair in a manbun while at work he assumed I was part of his tribe.

He assumed wrong.

"Fucking hell, Mike. I can't believe how fucking dead it is. Mum may as well not even bother opening past five o'clock. I keep telling her she'd be best to just focus on the café side of things."

"Yeah. It's pretty quiet."

"Quiet? That's an understatement. A morgue would have more life than this."

I could tell Chad was itching to have a conversation to help alleviate his boredom, but I didn't pursue it. I'd already endured nearly an hour's worth of stories about his nine-week trip to Sri Lanka last summer. "Yeah man," he'd said. "I don't think you can truly find yourself until you go on that sort of spiritual journey. A beautiful place. Beautiful people." Five minutes later he'd then described how after his Sri Lanka trip he'd stopped off at Sydney on his way home to New Zealand where he'd "banged three bitches in one weekend!" That of course then saw me forced into a high-five I wanted no part of.

I had bit my tongue, knowing if I snapped at him for being a douchebag then I'd probably wind up getting fired by his mum. This was my third job in less than a year after giving previous managers a piece of my mind.

I think part of the problem was people often misjudged me. Based on appearances I came across like some cruisy, shy introvert with a penchant for grunge music. A little shabby perhaps, but harmless. And in many ways that's the sort of person I was. But that didn't mean I couldn't stand up for myself. It could be a schoolyard bully, a psycho teacher, or a manager on an ego trip. I never shied away from calling out bullshit—usually to my own detriment as evidenced by my history of school detentions and already checkered work history. Gavin sometimes joked that I'd make an excellent contestant on a reality show because I'd deliver good conflict. But he clarified that by saying the reason I attracted tension was because I had a strong moral compass and knew right from wrong. However, I suspect several teachers and former co-workers would probably say I was just a moody cunt.

The truth was it may have been a bit of both.

The bar came alive again when three girls walked into the bar. I recognised them from high school, which I'd only graduated from three months prior. The girls were from a popular clique, each one atop of the social pyramid based on their looks, but it was the brunette in the middle who grabbed my attention, and Chad's too I imagine. Her name was Janine Halcomb. She was gorgeous. A tiny little thing, maybe five-feet-two, with a body for days—stretched tight inside of a red tank top and painted-on jean shorts. Her legs weren't long, but the open-toed stilettos she wore made up for her lack of height, giving her at least four inches, those calves sculpted and tan—satiny-smooth and coated with some type of shimmer oil.

Her dark hair was pinned up into a retro flip, her red lips matched the plunging top she wore, showing off those tits that had starred in countless school boy fantasies. It was little wonder she'd been the most popular girl at school and had dated the most popular boy, Hayden Jones. I'd heard she was single again after Hayden had left for university. Janine didn't need a degree to get a good job. I'd heard she'd gone to work for her father's accounting firm instead, probably starting in the same role and on the same pay as someone who'd spent three years studying for a degree.

"Good evening, ladies," Chad greeted them. "What can I get you to drink?"

Within seconds of them ordering their drinks, Chad morphed from slacker son working in his mother's bar to Tom Cruise in Cocktail, mixing drinks with a skill and flair I didn't even know he had.

Knowing my presence was not required, or wanted, I went out back to the kitchen and wiped the benches down for the second time this shift. While the latest round of cleaning was pointless, it was good to busy myself with something to do. The moment I wasn't doing anything, my mind would wander to Brian and I'd get sad with how it felt like I'd been ghosted by my best friend. I kept trying to think if there was something I had done to upset him, but I couldn't think of anything. But the more I thought about it the more I understood how Brian's sudden decision to attend university may not have actually been all that sudden. It would have explained why he'd been distant the past few months, probably worried how I would react to the news.

When he did finally tell me, only a week before leaving, I'd responded with my usual numbness to feeling abandoned. As shocked as I had been to know I was losing my best friend to Auckland, I can't say I was completely surprised. A boy like Brian had probably always been destined to study law like both his parents had. But I had genuinely believed him when he'd told me he didn't want to do that, telling me his plan was to get a job at one of the banks in town and climb the ladder the old-fashioned way.

Brian Quayle and I had known each other since primary school where we had bonded through being the black sheep on the playground. I was the snotty-nosed kid from the wrong side of the tracks and Brian was the nerdy four-eyed asthmatic obsessed with Lego and spaceships. An only child to two prominent lawyers, Brian was doted on by his wealthy parents who considered him a miracle baby after the trouble they'd had conceiving. This had been awesome for me because whenever I'd stay at his house I'd get to experience the good life not found in my neighbourhood. But that wasn't why I liked Brian. I liked him because he was sweet, kind and a total fucking dork who could make me laugh unintentionally.

It wasn't until intermediate that our duo became a trio when we welcomed Jockey into the fold, much to Mr and Mrs Quayle's disproval. The runty Savage boy had been held back a year but that still put him in the year above us. For the first time in our lives, Brian and I had found someone officially uncooler than us and—better yet—Jockey constantly told us how awesome we were. Despite Jockey's compliments boosting our egos, the taint of unpopularity stayed with each of us throughout our schooling. Jockey of course confirmed his loser status when he dropped out at sixteen, and Brian and I would go onto graduate still known as oddballs, labelled collectively as the Kurt Cobain wannabe and Lego freak.

Secretly, I had harboured a small crush on my best friend ever since he'd raced through puberty a whole year ahead of me. It was as if he had gone to bed a boy and woke up the next just a moustache away from manhood. After that, I found myself taking more notice of him, like the times I'd discreetly watch him while we'd get changed for gym class. Brian was always blissfully unaware of me scoping out the bulge in his underwear, or how I admired the tufts of hair under his arms. The crush was just a private little thing I kept to myself—as I did with any male who caught my sexual attention—but this crush was special because I felt like I knew a secret others didn't—and I don't mean the fact I wanted to play with his dick. It was because I knew just how sexy Brian Quayle actually was. While most people at school dismissed him as the nerd obsessed with Lego, I knew that beneath his iron-pressed jeans, ugly sweaters and spectacles, was a handsome face and a body rivalling any of the popular boys.

I'd had numerous chances to make a move on him through the years, like the many times we'd shared a bed when staying at each other's home, but I never did make a move. I wasn't an idiot and knew that any move would be swiftly rejected. Brian was straight in the most conservative of ways, about as old-fashioned as the sweaters he liked to wear. He would have been horrified to think another boy would want to touch his dick, especially if he knew that boy were me.

Shrill laughter floated into the kitchen from the bar and I could tell that Chad must have been flirting his ass off with Janine and her friends. Blocking them out, I fetched my pocket from my pocket and navigated my way to Brian's Instagram page. There were two new pictures; one of the Auckland skyline taken from the window of his dorm, the other showed him sat with an Indian boy as they nursed shots of tequila. Brian's mousy brown hair looked recently cut, his blue eyes making a rare appearance glassless. Without the corrective lenses, there was a fractional inward turn of the left that struck me as endearing, as well as oddly sexy. If it weren't for the t-shirt emblazoned with the periodic table on the front you'd almost forget you were looking at a guy who still collected Lego and who once knitted his own sweater for fun.

"You bastard," I muttered, angry at him for having fun without me.

To try and make myself feel better, I scrolled through his older pictures until I found one of the two of us together. I clicked on a favourite of mine, a picture from six months ago when Brian and I had gone fishing with his parents on his father's yacht. It wasn't a small yacht either, large enough that the family had sailed to Tonga on it the previous summer. Brian and I were sat on the deck, a bucket of ice by our bare feet. I saw the way our knees were touching, his hairy calf resting against mine. I swallowed nervously, while at the same time feeling my arousal spike.

I looked at the comments people had left, the top one from Jockey saying **Looking good boys.** In response to Jockey's comment Fiona, who had been dating Jockey at the time, had written, *My man sure has some handsome friends xx*

I remember wondering at the time if Jockey had been pissed off with his girlfriend for writing that. He had never said anything about it, but then I don't suppose he would have told us if it did annoy him. But I do remember Brian going on and fucking on about Fiona's comment, insisting she had a thing for him.

"She's like that with everyone," I'd said to him.

"I don't think so. You should see the way she looks at me. Like she wants me."

"If you say so."

Brian had never admitted it but I knew he was jealous of Jockey dating the older woman. He would keep saying how he couldn't understand why someone as hot as Fiona would date a loser like our army-obsessed friend. I didn't get it either but I also didn't consider

Fiona the goddess that Brian and Jockey clearly did. Sure she was pretty, and I wouldn't have said no, but I'd never sullied a sock in her honour.

Brian though, he'd received that honour a few times.

I swiped the screen and brought up other pictures from that fishing trip, including one of Brian with his shirt off. Broad-shouldered and smooth-chested, he was more muscular than the baggy t-shirts and ugly sweaters he often wore suggested. The strip of hair beneath his belly button plunged beneath the hemline of his shorts, going places I wished I had visited. My cock punched against my jeans, as if it was trying to get out. I was almost tempted to whip my dick out and cum right over Brian's smiling mug to teach him a lesson.

"Guess who got himself a phone number."

The masculine, but naturally lilting voice drifted from the kitchen doorway behind me. Shoving the phone back in my pocket, I turned to see Chad smirking triumphantly. "I'm guessing that would be you," I responded.

"You bet. The Chadster is a hit with the young ones." He suddenly glanced in the direction of my crotch, then smiled with a more than lecherous gleam in his eye. "No one told me the circus was in town?"

"What?"

He stepped over and gave my cock a tap. "You're pitching a tent, bro." Another tap. "A major one."

"Oi, stop touching my dick."

Chad laughed. "Settle down. You don't have the bits and piece I'm into. My boarding school days are well behind me. And that was only out of necessity."

I started blushing for both of us.

"You should go have a quick tug in the toilets," he suggested. "I do it all the time. It's hard to focus at work when you're boned up that bad." His gaze found its way back to my dick that wasn't deflating as fast as I'd like. "And you look boned up in a bad way, brother."

I willed a sinkhole to open under Chad's feet. "I'm fine."

"Well, if you change your mind, you know what to do."

In a bid to change the topic, fast, I asked, "So which one gave you her number?"

"The brunette."

"Janine?"

"Is that her name?" Chad nodded. "You know her?"

"We went to school together. We were in the same English class."

"Cool. So does she put out?"

"How would I know?"

Chad shrugged. "Just thought a stud like you might have had a bash on that door."

"That's one door I have not tried knocking on."

"Speaking of doors," Chad said, "did I tell you about the time I went to the monastery in Romania? The doors on the place were older than New Zealand. Can you imagine that? Doors that have been around longer than an entire country."

Fearing another long tale from The Adventures of Chad, I interrupted him and said, "You know what... I think I will go have that wank."

Chapter 6

THE NEXT DAY SAW ME waste the morning playing videogames before spending a couple hours in the afternoon working on my latest novel; a murder mystery set in 1920s New Zealand. It had taken me two months to outline the plot and conjure up twists to throw readers off who the murderer was. Since then I had written twelve of the planned thirty chapters, but it was proving tough to push through the story.

Unfortunately, burying myself in a fictional world of my own creation wasn't distracting me the way it had when I wrote my first book when Mum had run off. Whenever I had tried working on my latest story, a certain word or image would remind me of Brian and I'd find myself getting angry, and then horny as I began to picture his face, his sexy little nipples, his hairy legs, and the cock of his I'd never had a chance to properly lay eyes on. That's when I'd find myself abandoning the story and going to lay down on my bed for a wank while I imagined myself hatefucking Brian in the ass.

And it had just happened again, resulting in me panting on my bed with my jeans at my ankles, a warm pool of come on my belly.

Wiping the mess up with a dirty sock, I decided I needed to get out of the house. That meant a trip to town to go shopping at Moa Hill's one and only mall. I had no idea what it was I wanted to buy, but I'd just been paid and the money was burning a hole in my pocket. Without Brian here anymore, nagging at me about the importance of saving, I was free to be a bit frivolous. Although I earned bugger all from my job, I also had bugger all expenses. Gavin only charged me fifty dollars board so that usually left me with a couple hundred each week to blow on whatever I wanted—despite Brian's lectures.

When I reached the mall an hour later, I saw that it was a pretty lazy weekday, not too much traffic along the tiled walkways that glowed softly from the sun streaming down through the skylights above. After buying myself a videogame and a new top, I decided to get something to eat in the food court. I took a table off to the side. As I was munching on fries and reading an advertising pamphlet someone had left on the table, I started getting the feeling that I was being watched.

I glanced around and saw Brian's parents sat at a table about thirty feet away. Judging by the corporate clothes they had on it looked like the pair had just finished work. Mrs Quayle smiled and waved, encouraging me to come over. She was looking elegant as always, the only member in the family with any clue about fashion. Her dyed-blond hair and stylish blouse made her look much younger than her real age of fifty-five. At sixty, Rowan Quayle was five years older than his beautiful wife and looked more his age courtesy of his salt and pepper hair and weathered face.

Collecting my fries and bag of shopping, I made my way over to sit with them.

"Fancy seeing you here," Brian's mother said. "I was just telling Rowan how it was odd we hadn't recognised anyone yet. I'm forever usually bumping into someone I know."

"That's because you're too much of a social butterfly, Ingrid," Mr Quayle said in a mock-stern tone. "Everybody knows you."

"I suppose that happens when you win Moa Hill's lawyer of the year three years running," she teased.

The pair had a friendly rivalry with their law professions, with Mrs Quayle the more successful of the two. She'd even been on television a couple times from her involvement with high profile cases.

"What have you been up to, Michael?" she asked. "I'm missing you almost as much as Brian. It's strange you not coming over each day."

"I've just been busy with work. Same old."

"You're working at Chaos, is that right?" Mr Quayle asked.

"That's the one."

"It's a nice place that," he said, like his opinion was of the upmost importance. "I met a client there for lunch last week. Great coffee and the food wasn't bad. I don't recall seeing you there though."

"I'm only part time at the moment."

"Really?" Mr Quayle cleared his throat and sat up straighter. "Shouldn't you be working forty hours a week now that you're no longer at school? Or have you decided to study online?"

I tried to hold his eyes as long as I could. Lasted only a couple of seconds. "Uh..."

"You're far too smart to be wasting your brains," he said, adjusting his glasses. "I know Brian was jealous of the grades you got. A young man like yourself could have a very bright future if—"

"Leave him alone, Rowan," Mrs Quayle snapped at her husband. "Mike has plenty of time to decide what he wants to do. It's not like you and I didn't take gap years."

"Yeah," I mumbled. "It's a gap year." *No it's not.*

This got the pair started down memory lane, taking turns in telling me about their gap year; Mrs Quayle backpacked around Europe while Mr Quayle did a road trip around Australia.

While Mr Quayle began to tell us about being chased by a kangaroo, I couldn't help but smile at how much he reminded me of my best friend. If you wanted to know what Brian would look like in forty years then you only had to look at his drippy father wearing a stiff button-down shirt and a huge, shiny watch peeking out from the cuff to see what the future held. And it wasn't all bad, aside from the thinning grey hair and crow's feet. Father and son looked remarkably similar; bright blue eyes and bashful smiles that were warm and endearing. Mr Quayle was thinner than Brian, the man's obsession with cycling giving him a rangier physique than that of his son but otherwise the apple hadn't fallen far from the dorky tree.

"You must come have dinner with us one evening," Mrs Quayle said when her husband's kangaroo tale had ended. "Just because Brian isn't living at home doesn't mean you have to be a stranger."

"I'll be sure to pop over some time."

"Please do. You know Rowan and I both think very highly of you."

"By the way," Mr Quayle said. "We'll be going up to see Bri at the end of the month to see how he's settling in. Maybe you'd like to join us? Could be a fun day trip."

That perked me up. "If it's okay with Brian then sure."

"Why wouldn't it be okay with Brian?" Mrs Quayle looked confused. "I'm sure he's missing you like crazy. You two have been inseparable for years."

I was tempted to tell them how their son had been ignoring me but I knew better than to be so bratty. Besides, it wasn't like they could do anything about it. Brian was an adult—just—and was allowed to ignore who he wanted.

"Anyway my dear," Mr Quayle said to his wife. "I better get going. You know how angry Andrew gets if I'm late to play squash."

"Tell Andrew I would appreciate it if he lets you win. You always come home in a bad mood when you lose."

"That's not a bad mood, it's my competitive spirit, which I believe is part of my appeal." He patted his chest and let out a low rumble. "And my manly muscles of course."

She chuckled. "Keep telling yourself that, Rowan."

Brian's father gave his wife a kiss then walked away, his long strides moving fast as if he were already running late.

Mrs Quayle and I chatted for a few more minutes before she too said she had to get going. "It was nice seeing you, Michael. And make sure you come for dinner soon. I mean it. I consider you part of the family."

I smiled and assured her that I would. Sat alone eating my fries, I couldn't help but feel sadder about Brian after hearing his mother refer to me as family. That just made what he was doing feel so much worse.

I WAS HALFWAY HOME from town when I found myself busting for a piss. Cursing the frozen coke I'd ordered after eating my fries, I knew I wouldn't make it home in time so decided to make a detour to the nearest park. I wasn't thrilled about it because the park in question was Hickford Park and it was starting to get dark.

Hickford Park, a scraggly patch of land separating a residential neighbourhood from a dilapidated business district, had a reputation. It was occupied by pot-smoking teens during the day, men on the prowl at night, and had often found itself in the crime section of the local newspaper. Most recently there had been a spate of muggings committed by someone the paper had named The Demon Granny Basher. It was sensationalist bullshit taken from a grain of truth. Some Polynesian dude covered in tattoos was mugging elderly people in the area, and not just grannies. Granddads too. The lowlife wore a devil's play mask to hide his identity when sneaking up behind his elderly victims and snatching their purses or wallets. The story would have been a non-event had it not been for the fact the last victim had suffered a heart attack and died. That had been three weeks ago but the story was still the talk of the town.

As the park came into view, I saw that the time had gone from stoner o'clock to cocksucking hours. Already, in the early evening, I could see the men gathering. Some sat in their cars, waiting to see what happened by, while others wandered the grounds, trolling. Across the park, near the restrooms, a man in white shorts did a slow stroll within a circle of light cast from a lamppost in front of the squat cinder-block building. Another man, in blue jeans and a black T-shirt, leaned against the building, one foot hitched up against the wall, smoking a cigarette, ignoring the guy in white shorts and looking at me approaching the park.

"I'm not interested fellas," I muttered under my breath.

I may not have been opposed to getting it on with another dude but like hell I would do it with a man who frequented here. No one wanted to be known as a Hickford Homo—the term branded on any guy stupid enough to get caught cruising this park. A couple years ago a spiteful homophobe, hiding under the guise of being a "concerned resident", began secretly recording the men who frequented the park, taking their pictures and then putting them on a website they'd created called—you guessed it—Hickford Homos. The website was short lived but I gather it damaged many lives and led to several marriages ending. One boy at school, Isaac Fraser, was one of the unlucky sods to find his face on the website and it had made his life at school a living hell. So while the website that outed him may have been long gone the name would never leave him. He and the others would forever be known in town as Hickford Homos.

Knowing this, I decided immediately to make my way to a group of trees away from the toilets to take my much-needed piss then skedaddle my ass out of here. My imagination was running wild as I snuck into the bushes, keeping an eye out for demon granny bashers, homosexual rapists and homophobic vigilantes.

There was just enough light left in the dusking sky piercing the treetops to allow me to see where I was going. A few metres into the forested patch, I found an oak tree with my piss's name on it. I glanced around and saw a man leaning against a tree, about twenty feet away. He was significantly older than me, maybe early or mid-forties, and very slender, with short blonde hair. He had a smug, confident look on his face that was, frankly, intimidating.

For fuck sake, I thought. But my need to pee was too strong to worry about some voyeur watching from afar.

I looked back down at my jeans, fumbling to open my zipper and pull my cock out. My palms were sweaty, my throat felt dry, my heart was pounding, and my cock... was getting hard.

Fuck!

It felt like several minutes had passed, but it was probably only a handful of seconds before my peeping Tom came and joined me. His cocky smile was omnipresent as he looked me over.

"I'm only here to take a piss, dude," I said, deepening my voice to try and sound hard. "So don't get any funny ideas."

"Do you mind if I watch?" he asked, in a way that implied he really did not care what my answer might be.

"I'm taking a piss."

"I know. And I would like to watch."

"Fine," I said, trying to play it cool. "But don't touch me."

"I'm Simon," he said, his eyes locked on my penis. "You're pretty hot."

I could feel the blush flooding my cheeks. I couldn't meet his gaze. Instead, I stared at the base of the V-neck collar of his sweater.

"Is someone a little pee shy?" he said with a touch of mirth. "That's cool. I can handle that."

"There's nothing to handle. I'm only here to take a piss."

"Then piss...or am I making you too hard to go?"

Part of my mind was screaming in my head, telling me I should be insulted. But that part was small, dominated by the feelings of sexual curiosity that now roared through my brain like an inferno.

"Hey, don't be embarrassed," Simon said, stepping closer. "Mine's not that big either."

I felt a spark of defensiveness. "My dick's not small."

He shrugged. "Of course not."

I heard him sigh with anticipation, watched his hands drop to his slacks. The bulge of his cock was just visible through the material, but the more he groped the more visible it became. There was something about Simon that I didn't like, or maybe it was just that I didn't like the way his presence was turning me on.

He reached inside his fly, fumbled around a bit, and pulled out his cock. It wasn't very hard at first, but as soon as the air hit it, it began angling upward. Soft-looking blonde hair sprouted around the base of his dick. It also covered his balls, but sparsely, which I noticed as he extracted them from his pants.

So there I was, staring at another man's cock. A cock I had no desire to see. I contemplated moving to a different tree but figured Simon would just follow after me. That's when I felt my urine sting the base of my dick and the floodgates began to open.

I knew it would be a big piss and I just hoped I'd be finished before any of the other Hickford Homos came to watch, and that Simon kept his frisky hands to himself.

When my piss reached full-force, hissing and splattering against the trunk of the tree, Simon stuck his hand out, wetting his palm with my urine, drenching the gold band on his wedding finger.

"What the fuck, dude? That's gross."

He ignored me, watching his hand intently as I drowned it in liquid. Then he shuffled closer, sticking his now-hard cock in the direct path of my yellow torrent. "That's it, sexy. Cover my cock with your *pisss*," he whispered encouragingly, clinging to that s.

I felt dirty, like he was dragging me into an act I had no desire to commit, but I was locked in for the whole dirty ride and would not be leaving this spot until my bladder was empty.

I don't know how long it took, felt like ages, but eventually my bladder was empty and I shook away the last few dribbles before zipping my dick back up.

Simon stroked his saturated cock slowly; an expression of triumph mixed with arousal on his slightly lined face. Then, to my horror, he began to lick the piss from his hand, sucking each finger into his mouth. He gave me a wink. An invitation.

"You're a freak," I said.

"And you my dear boy taste delicious."

I shook my head in disgust and got out of there while he cackled like a witch who'd just poured a secret ingredient into a cauldron. My feet weren't used to running, but they were running right now, across the field and past the carpark. I was in such a rush to get away that I didn't even stop to look back at the parked black Mercedes with the number plate **QUAYLE.**

Chapter 7

"THAT IS FUCKING HILARIOUS." Jockey burst out laughing. "Tell me it again."

"I've already told you the story three times. It doesn't change."

Sat in the raggedy-ass armchair near Jockey's computer, I watched as my stoner pal laughed so hard he almost fell off the couch he was perched on. If he laughed any louder then I was sure his aunt and uncle would come out soon and tell him to shut the fuck up. I know I was tempted to.

What he found so hilarious was of course the retelling of my experience taking a piss at Hickford Park. I hadn't been stupid enough to share the part about seeing Brian's father's car parked there. I didn't want to start a rumour that was most likely not true.

There's bound to be an innocent explanation.

Most people knew what happened at that park after dark and I was sure Mr Quayle wouldn't knowingly park there if that's what he had gone there to do——which I'm sure he hadn't. The most likely explanation was that the squash club he played at was nearby, which would explain him being in the area. The alternative was too grim to entertain, which was probably why I had not looked online to see if there was a squash court nearby. I didn't care how much Mr

Quayle looked like his son, there was no way I wanted to imagine a man who'd recently turned sixty sucking dick.

"Did it turn you on?" Jockey asked when he'd finished hyperventilating from his laughter. "Pissing on the dude's cock."

"What do you think?" I said accusingly.

"I dunno. That's why I'm asking."

"The answer is no."

"Really?" Jockey looked surprised. "I reckon it would have tuned me on a little bit. The dominance of it. Like you're marking a weaker man as your territory."

The socially acceptable response to that would have been to mock the shit out of him, call him a homo, and had Brian been here that's exactly what I would have done, but instead I nodded and agreed with him. What Jockey said made sense, and may have explained why I had found myself turned on at the time despite Simon not being my type.

"Have you ever watched any of those Hickford Homo videos online?" Jockey asked. "I watched one last week and it was fucking hilarious."

"I thought the site was taken down?"

"It was but the videos keep popping up online in different places. I highly recommend watching them if you're keen for a laugh. There's something hella funny about watching a dude trying to run away from a camera when his pants are around his ankles."

I was tempted to ask what sort of sites he was looking at but decided I'd rather not know. "I think my one lived experience is enough. I don't need to see any more of their mating rituals."

Jockey sprawled out on the couch, one pants-clad leg draping up over the back, the other dangling down. The army-style jacket he had on was open, gravity tugging the down side toward the floor, giving me a good view of his tanned chest, the tit on the right pec, the top of his pubes curling out from the vee made when he undid the button holding his pants together under his hair-haloed navel.

The image was more sexual than it had any right to be. But I wondered if that came with the territory considering he'd sucked my dick for two years. Even though it was all done under the guise of a bro-job arrangement, I felt there was a very thin line separating us between that and something that ran much deeper. I would have talked with him about it but I was afraid of what his answer might be. He may not have been a Hickford Homo but I was just as terrified of feeling cornered by him if my suspicions were true that he liked our arrangement a little too much.

"Oh my God, I'm so horny. My nuts feel like sandbags weighing my dick down!" he announced out of the blue like a man unable to restrain any thought that passed through his mind. "I've already used the Fleshlight twice since I got home from work."

"Thanks for the overshare."

"It's been so fucking long since I've had any action that I find myself getting hard just from a breeze licking my balls." He reached inside his pants and gave his balls a good scratch. "It's days like this I miss Fiona. I could have just dumped a load in her and been good."

"And to think she broke up with such a gentleman," I said, heavy with the sarcasm.

"Speaking of being a gentleman." He lowered his leg from the back of the couch and rolled onto his side. "Have you thought about doing what I asked for my birthday?"

And there it was again. That lingering vibe of sexual interest that made my tummy do squirmy things.

"Not really."

"My birthday is this Saturday, dog. That's only five days away."

"I know that."

"Well... you know how badly I want my birthday dare."

"But it's weird."

"How is it weird?"

"How is it not weird?" My voice came out shrill. "You want to tie me to a chair and stick a pump to my dick."

"Yeah, but it'll be fun. For both of us. Honestly, you'll cum bucket loads, bro."

I glanced in the direction of his utility room. "Has it arrived yet?"

"Not yet. It should be here tomorrow or the next day. I can't wait. You're gonna love it. I've almost finished making the chair to go with it. I'll make sure to sand it down a bit more yet. Don't want you getting a splinter in your ass."

"There's no risk of that happening because I'm probably not even gonna do it."

"But we always do dares for one another on our birthdays. That's what this is... a dare. That should make you feel less weird about it."

"It doesn't."

His mouth down-turned, threatening an A-grade sulk. "Remember when you dared me to run naked around the school quad for your birthday? I did that for you."

"To be fair, that was mostly Brian's idea, not mine."

"So?"

"So you got suspended for a week. It wasn't exactly the main float at the good idea parade."

Jockey shrugged. "Right, but I still did it."

I chewed the inside of my cheek. I couldn't remember the last time I'd seen Jockey so adamant I do something for him. He was usually chill and didn't ask for anything other than my company.

"Let me get this straight," he said bitterly, "it's okay for you and Brian to make me do stupid shit I'm not thrilled about but when the shoe is on the other foot it's a different story. Well then... thanks for letting me know how *not* appreciated I am." Man, Jockey was really laying it on thick.

Rubbing my face with my hands, I tried to think of a reasonable excuse. Something even my sex-obsessed childhood buddy couldn't argue with. Problem was, all I kept coming back to was the simple fact that... I just didn't want to do it.

I started to feel bad when I saw how disappointed he looked. With his lips all pouty and his head recently shorn down to a number three all over, he resembled a child with cancer who'd just been told Lady Gaga wasn't coming to sing to him at the hospital.

Stop making me feel so fucking guilty!

Accompanying my guilt was the knowledge that as of this moment Jockey Savage was the only real friend I had. And while I doubted he would end our friendship if I said no to being his kinky lab rat, I also didn't want there to be any tension between us. I needed Jockey now more than ever.

"Brian would have done the dare," Jockey whispered sulkily. "He wouldn't have liked it, but he would have done it. But I suppose that's because he's a real friend."

"For fuck's sake," I sighed. "I'll do it. But on the condition we never talk about it afterwards and you tell no one. The last thing I want is people finding out I let you watch me get milked like a cow."

"You're the best, Mike. Thank you!" Jockey bounced forward all smiley like he hadn't just poured an entire bottle of guilt sauce over me. "You won't regret this. I promise."

But within two minutes I was regretting my decision when Jockey informed me that for the machine to work properly, I would have to not cum until his birthday—five days away!

"You seriously expect me to go five days without wanking?" I snorted derisively. "You're dreaming, buddy."

"I've done it before. It's easy."

"Bullshit." I eyed him suspiciously. "You're the horniest bastard I know. There's no way you could go that long without playing with yourself."

"I didn't have a choice."

"I don't recall you ever breaking both your wrists."

He laughed and shook his head. "Nar, bro. Come with me and I'll show you what I mean." Jockey walked over to the bookcase and picked up a set of keys. He turned back to see I was still sat down. "Coming?"

Begrudgingly, I got up and followed him into the bathroom where he used the keys to unlock the door to his utility room. My annoyance died down somewhat, curious to get my first look inside the room in over two years. It was pitch-black and the musty smell of forgotten treasure filled my nose. My eyes spasmed in shock when Jockey flicked the light on, temporarily blinding me. When my eyes adjusted to the harsh white light, I looked around and recognised some of the army gear and old childhood toys I'd seen the last time I'd been in here. But there was much more filling the shelves now. Much more adult things; like the ropes and chains I had suspected. But there was other stuff too; rolls of material, PVC mostly, red and black. A couple dildos, possibly of the vibrating variety. Nipple clamps. Handcuffs. I also noticed several pairs of women's knickers and men's boxers.

"This place is like a fucking sex shop," I exclaimed.

"That's all the stuff I bought while I was dating Fiona. I told you she was a kinky bitch."

"So are you by the looks."

"I bought most of this shit for her, not me. But I figured I'd hold onto it cos you never know when I might meet another woman like her."

"*Riiight.*"

"Anyway," he said as he turned around to the other wall of shelves. "I brought you in here to show you this."

I watched his hand pick up what looked like a plastic tube with a tiny padlock attached. Upon closer inspection I realised the tube was shaped like a cock.

I looked to him and said, "Is that what I think it is?"

"It sure is." Jockey lowered the device and dangled it in front of his crotch. "It's a cock cage. That's how I went a whole week without playing with the little fella."

"Why would you want to wear something like that?"

"This is a bit embarrassing but when Fiona and I first got together I was a bit quick to finish the deed...if you know what I mean. She made me wear it so I could learn to last longer, and be less selfish in bed. It worked wonders. No shit. I'm a fucking stallion now because of this thing, and not afraid to get my tongue stuck deep into a pussy."

A part of me wanted to laugh like a little kid but the adult part of my brain understood that Jockey was sharing something very personal with me and it wasn't a laughing matter. "How long did you use it for?"

"On and off for about four months. I wasn't in it the whole time. Just four or five days at a time. But like I said, it worked."

"Wow..." I lifted my gaze from the chastity device to meet his brown eyes. "I can't believe you did that for her."

He shrugged like it was no big deal then handed me the cock cage. I hesitated, not keen to touch something he'd worn on his dick. "Take it, Mike. It's clean. It's been washed thoroughly."

Gingerly, I accepted the kinky object, unable to fathom how a man could fit his junk inside something so confined. So restrictive.

"It might be a little big for you but it should still fit."

I raised an eyebrow at him. "What do you mean a little big for me?"

"My dick is bigger than yours," he said flatly. "Fiona ordered the cage based on my measurements."

I wanted to be offended but I could tell he wasn't saying it to be rude.

Pointing behind me, he said, "You might wanna go in the bathroom and rub one out before you put it on."

"Why?"

"You won't be able to wank for five days, doofus."

"Oh..." I nodded slowly, mesmerized by the tiny prison in my hand. "I guess that would make sense."

Jockey escorted me out of the utility room and locked it up again. He gave me a quick explanation as to how to put the contraption on—which I needed—then wished me a good wank before giving me a flirty wink and closing the bathroom door.

Lowering my jeans, I closed my eyes and stroked my cock, trying to think about anything other than the fact that just outside the bathroom door Jockey was sitting, waiting for me to emerge with my dick padlocked inside a plastic tube. I had to wipe that from my mind and think about something that would make me hard.

I conjured up one of my Brian fantasies. The one where I imagined making a move on him while he slept beside me in my bed. I'd got off on this many times, probably because it was something I very nearly did one night after we'd got drunk together on tequila.

In reality it had only gone as far as me reaching over and touching his firm, hairy thigh while he slept. My fingers had dared to graze the warm mound of his cock and balls encased in his underwear but that's when guilt had stuck me like lightening and I'd let go and jerked off in quiet without him knowing.

In my fantasy, however, guilt never struck, and I would do much more than touch my best friend's thigh and graze his balls. I had revisited the scenario many times since then, until it was so familiar that I could reliably predict where in the fantasy I would shoot my load. It generally happened a minute or two after Brian, aroused by the ministrations of my tongue, begged me to fuck him good and hard. I was relieved to find that the fantasy was once again doing its trick. My dick had stiffened almost immediately upon picturing Brian, his legs spreading to welcome me into his warmth.

Now my hand moved quickly up and down my shaft, coaxing an orgasm from my balls. With practiced skill, I imagined the taste of Brian's dick as I began to suck him off, felt the weight of his long fingers on my head as Brian, realising what was going on, accepted the offer of release.

I was making love with Brian. Not the way men did in porn movies, detached and interested only in getting off, but in the way lovers did, with deliberate slowness so that the pleasure lingered and release was the happy by-product and not just the end result. I felt Brian's mouth move over my skin, his hands and tongue working together to coax joy from my body. I heard his breath, and smelled his sweat.

I was almost there. My breathing quickened, and I felt a tightening in my groin.

"Are you okay in there? Do you want to use my laptop to watch some porn on?"

The sound of Jockey's voice startled me. "I'm fine," I called out, horrified that Jockey actually seemed to be timing me.

I stopped jacking off and groaned. I'd been so close. But now I leaned back against the shower and sighed. Then I spotted out the corner of my eye a pair of green y-fronts in the laundry hamper near the door. There was only one person they could belong to and it made my stomach wobble, but it also brought on a perverse need.

Desperate times call for desperate measures...

As I shoved the whiffy material to my nose, I decided it was only right to honour the man whose ball sweat I was sniffing by casting him as the star of my fantasy. Jockey was not my type, but he did have one feature I had admired numerous times: that sexy ass of his. It was beautiful and firm, a little bit hairy but utterly fuckable.

Unlike the passionate lovemaking I'd just fantasised with Brian, I replaced it with brutal sodomy as I pictured Jockey bent over the end of his bed and taking every inch of my cock, hard, harder than hard, so hard he was whimpering and begging for me to stop.

I didn't stop though. I just slapped his ass, told him to shut the fuck up and take it. And he did. Took every thrust I gave him until I—

"Oh fuck..." I bit down the tail end of a grunt. "Fuck."

I quickly covered my dick with his undies, spoofing into the rancid material. My body shook and shivered from the intense release, my balls emptying every drop of sperm I had been carrying around with me today. If I was about to go five days without another wank, this was a good one to start my famine on.

Burying the corrupted briefs at the bottom of his laundry hamper, I then gave my dick a quick wash in the hand basin and went about putting the device on. Following Jockey's instructions, I slipped the ring on over my penis and behind my scrotum, so the ring was against my body. Then, I placed the cage over my limp cock, making sure the locking pins and holes lined up. They connected. There was a little bit of room left around my dick but nowhere near enough to allow an erection. Finally, closing my eyes as if I were about to get an injection, I turned the key and removed it from the locking cylinder.

Through the one eye that dared to look, I assessed my new predicament. Locked and secure. It felt weird but not as uncomfortable as I had feared. Just foreign. Like my dick had turned into a robot.

Robo-cock. That made me chuckle.

Pulling my jeans up, I opened the door and walked out to find Jockey waiting for me on the couch.

"How's it fit?" he asked when he saw me standing there. "Snug as a bug in a rug?"

"Something like that," I mumbled.

"Can I see?"

I'd been expecting this request, which was why I hadn't zipped up my fly. Lowering the denim material, I flashed him my now imprisoned cock. Jockey came over to get a closer look. "It's a better fit than I expected. Good shit."

"One size fits all apparently."

After taking the key from me, Jockey knelt down in front of my crotch, his breath swirling around my balls. When he spoke, he did so while staring at my caged cock. "Just a word of warning, you'll wanna sit down to piss. Trust me, it goes everywhere if you try pissing standing up. I learned that the hard way and ended up with piss stains all down my pants at work one day. Not fun. Also, you might wake up sore from nocturnal boners. That's normal. Just ignore it and go back to sleep. You'll get used to it."

"Great, now you tell me."

"You'll be fine, dog." Jockey gave my tube-clad cock a gentle pat. "You be a good boy, little Mike, and we'll let you out to play on Saturday."

Chapter 8

GAVIN HAD BEEN WALKING on sunshine all week, fuelled by his blossoming romance with Fiona. He'd dated several women since Mum had left but this was the first time he had appeared so smitten. I suppose Fiona was much better-looking than the other women he had dated, but I think the real reason for the man's dopey smile was the noises the pair were making each night in Gavin's bedroom. Whatever Fiona was doing to him in there she was doing it well.

To be honest, I had thought when Gavin found out Fiona was Jockey's ex that would have put an end to things. But Gavin didn't give a shit. Fiona had come clean to him three days ago about her past relationship with Jockey, telling Gavin how long she had dated the young man twelve years her junior. This was the part I'd been sure would rattle Gavin, reminding him about the age gap between my mum and him. But he thought nothing of it. And rather than be concerned as to whose sloppy seconds he was ploughing, Gavin had just found it funny, joking how Fiona must be grateful to be with a real man finally. He was so not bothered that he had even taken Fiona out for dinner to meet his best mate Trent and Trent's wife Donna. Gavin introducing a woman to his best mate was unheard of, which also probably meant Fiona had officially climbed above the rank of fuck buddy. I was happy that Gavin was happy but at the same time I couldn't help but be a little concerned.

While Gavin was in a fantastic mood, I was experiencing quite the opposite.

It had been four days since locking my cock up and I was well the fuck over it. I couldn't think about anything other than my cock, and the only thing I could do with it was stroke my balls. Sleep, especially for the first couple of nights, was nearly impossible. I'd wake up, my cock straining futilely against the cage. I'd get up to piss, and squirt all over myself, even sitting down. The other issue I had was a raging form of cock-envy.

Every guy I passed in the street had me jealously checking out their crotch, assuming they most likely had free dicks, able to touch themselves as much as they like. Not me. Any attempt to play with little Mike through the cage resulted in a fledgling hard-on that would squeeze against the walls of his prison and cause me to hiss in pain.

To avoid this cock-envy, I'd stayed at home when not at work and spent more time on writing my book. That was perhaps the one good thing to have come out of this. I had raced through two chapters each day and was now very close to finishing the first draft. My creative juices had been flowing so freely I had even penned a quick outline of what my next book would be. Unfortunately my creative juices hadn't been the only thing flowing these past four days. I may not have been able to climax properly but that hadn't stopped the build-up of precum seeping out of my horny dick, or the piss dribbles gathering inside the cage. I was pretty sure if I didn't have a wash soon my crotch would rival onions in the eye-watering department.

My concern about my hygiene had me calling Jockey this morning to tell him I needed the key so I could have a wash down there. To begin with he told me I was probably overreacting before eventually offering to come over after work and unlock me, but only on the condition he could supervise the shower.

"Why the hell do you need to supervise my shower?" I'd demanded.

"So I know you don't slip in a sneaky wank. I need your balls full for Saturday."

Rather than give him the satisfaction of exerting any more control over me than he already had, I'd told him I would just wait to wash my dick on Saturday.

After that phone call I'd returned to my room to work on my novel, only venturing out now that my stomach had started rumbling for food. However, as I entered the lounge on my way to the kitchen I was greeted with a sight that made me lose my appetite: Gavin sat in just his underwear while he clipped his toenails.

"Clipping the trotters, are we?"

"Yeah." Gavin's focus remained on his foot resting on the coffee table. "Fiona said they were too long."

"Does she want you to paint them too, Gavina?"

"Oi, don't be cheeky." *Clip*. "Gotcha ya bastard." He held the clipped nail up as if it were the spiked head of a rival war chief.

"Are you meeting up with her tonight?"

"Yeah. She's coming with me for a boardgame evening at Trent and Donna's." His face once again locked in concentration as he returned the clippers to his foot. "She said she'll call me to come pick her up after her Mum swings by to pick the kids up."

"Her mum looks after her kids a lot."

Clip. The piece of toenail flew off onto the carpet. "Yeah. Her and her mum are really close."

He was too distracted by lining up the clippers for the next piggy in line to detect my comment had been slightly barbed. Fiona dumping her kids off onto her mother had been a common occurrence when she was with Jockey and it had bugged me then too. I think the reason it rattled me was because it brought back memories of my Mum's dating life before she met Gavin, which hadn't been a fun time for me. Mind you, at least Fiona's kids got to stay with their grandmother, unlike me who'd been pawned off to anyone aged over twelve who would babysit for free.

When Gavin had finished prettying his hooves, and I knew I wasn't at risk of losing an eye from a ricocheting toenail, I went and sat beside him on the couch. "Cutting your toenails, taking her out for dinner...you must really like her."

"Fiona's a lot of fun."

"A lot of fun with three kids."

"You're bringing her kids up because...?"

"No reason. Just thought you'd realise that's a lot of baggage."

Gavin cocked a sceptical brow at me. "That's technically what you were if you look at it like that."

"Yeah, but there was just one of me, and I'm pretty fucking awesome."

"You are very that." He chuckled softly. "But I'm sure Fiona's kids are as well. Although I haven't actually met them yet"

That annoyed me. He still hadn't met these kids yet but was placing them on the same mantlepiece as me.

"I appreciate your concern, Mike, but it's all good. Fiona and I are fine. You don't need to worry about me and her *baggage*."

"When you say it like that you make me sound like an asshole."

"Maybe because it was an assholey thing to say. But it's okay. I suspect I know where it's coming from?"

Was my jealousy that obvious? My selfish need to not want to share the closest thing to a parent I have?

"You're just looking out for Jockey. I get it. I imagine he's probably told you to say something. Fiona tells me he's still into her in a big way, still texts her most days apparently, despite her telling him she ain't interested. If anything I feel sorry for the guy. He ain't likely to ever score a chick like her again. Tens and sevens don't go together. And you don't need me to tell you which is which."

I wasn't sure what surprised me more. Gavin thinking Fiona was a ten or that he considered Jockey a seven. "Shit. You're generous with the ratings. What am I?"

"A solid ten, of course. Same as me. We're probably the best-looking family on the whole street." He reached over and tucked an invisible strand of hair behind my ear. "But imagine how much hotter our household would be if you got a haircut."

That made me smile, mostly because he called us a family.

"So how did Jockey take the news when you told him I was seeing Fiona?"

"I haven't told him yet. I figured it's not my business."

"Oh." Gavin looked surprised. "Maybe that's a good thing. No need to rial the lad up if you don't need to. Shit, for all I know Fiona might give me the flick by next week."

"You think so?" My voice came out way too hopeful. "I mean, that would suck."

"Yeah, it would." Gavin bent his head forward and rubbed his eyebrows with his fingers. "But I don't think that's what she's planning on doing just yet. If my spidey senses are correct I've a feeling she might be around a lot longer yet."

And on those words *my* spidey senses jumped in front of a fast-moving bus.

FIONA CALLED GAVIN an hour later, and he raced out the door like Usain Bolt after a gold medal. It was nice to see him so happy, but it was also unsettling. Gavin's prediction Fiona and him would be an item for a long time worried me. Why? Because I guess even now I didn't feel totally secure in this nest. Gavin's house had been my home for more than a decade but I lived in fear that it could be taken away from me if he got serious with the wrong woman. And Fiona was very much the wrong woman. There was no way I could stay here if she and her three cum sprouts moved in. My ass would be out with the trash.

After finally fixing myself something to eat—reheated pizza from the night before—I settled down in the lounge again and flicked on Netflix. Despite the hundreds of shows and movies available there was fuck all I wanted to watch. My gaze wandered to above the television where Gavin's pride and joy hung on the wall: a framed All Black jersey signed by the legendary rugby player Sir Colin Meads. It was the only thing of value in the house, and I'm sure Gavin would have rescued it before saving me in the event of a fire. I remembered the day Colin Meads had died, we had been watching the news and after Gavin grumbled "That sucks" he'd then turned to Mum and me and said, "But can you imagine how much the jersey is worth now?"

While normal people may have had savings accounts and investments, Gavin was relying on this piece of rugby memorabilia to gain in value for his retirement. His other plan of course was to win big in the lottery, which is why he bought a ticket every pay day. He'd spend the week daydreaming aloud to anyone who would listen—which was usually only me—what he would spend the money on: a house, a boat, new car, holidays to the islands, and of course he'd use some of the money to finish off the work on Betsy. I remember the few times Brian had been here when Gavin would go on about winning lotto. My rich friend found it hilarious and told me in private what a fool Gavin was to even think he'd ever win lotto.

Maybe Gavin's optimism was laughable, but then I could hardly comment. I wasn't that good with money either and my pipe dreams of making a fortune as a published author were just as unlikely. But I think that's why I understood Gavin's lotto fantasy and happily talked with him about it. It was nice to dream, to talk about what could be if life was easier. I think that's something someone like Brian, who'd had everything handed to him, couldn't understand. The poor needed an escape just like everybody else. The difference was our escapes were usually found in fantasy—or addiction.

The more I thought about Brian's mocking of Gavin, the angrier it made me about him ghosting me. But I quickly reminded myself how kind Brian could be as well, generous to a fault, and up until moving away he'd always been inclusive. Well, he had been with me at least. It was probably that bundle of contradictions why

I'd always liked the snobby boy with a heart of gold a little more than a friend.

I dismissed my anger and thought back to that day on his father's yacht, the pair of us laughing and joking. Brian wandering around shirtless on deck while I discreetly checked out the faint outline of abs he had.

"*Hsst*." I winced as my dick tried hardening at the conjured image of a shirtless Brian.

"Settle down you," I scolded my cock. "You've only got to wait one more day."

My dick retreated like a frightened zoo animal while my stomach knotted at the thought of what tomorrow night might look like.

Chapter 9

TONIGHT WAS THE NIGHT.

Feet propped on the coffee table, I listened to the rattle of rain on the windows and thought about my impending visit to see Jockey. If the weather was an omen then I should have been alarmed. The rain had poured all day, becoming torrential in patches with flashes of sheet lightening and rumbling thunder. Still, I had no choice but to brave the elements if I wanted this tube off my cock.

We had talked on the phone this morning about how tonight would unfold. Jockey said he would text me tonight when he'd set up the machine, probably around seven, and tell me to come over. I was to be strapped to the chair, feet and hands cuffed, and endure two hours of "mind blowing bliss" according to Jockey. How mind blowing it would be remained to be seen but I had to admit I was sort of excited. Five days of not ejaculating will do that to guy. I was so worked up I would have gladly drilled a hole into a watermelon and fucked it.

Knowing that I would be fully naked in front of Jockey for the first time was a little intimidating. My Friday night visits to his sleepout only ever saw my pants falling to my ankles. Shit, I hadn't even taken off my shoes and socks in front of the guy before.

Similar to how the porn that would be playing acted like a shield so too did my shirt remaining on. It helped separate me from the act. While my lower half had a party in Jockey's mouth, my upper half had remained an innocent observer.

To help ease my nerves about being fully naked in front of my friend, I had spent way too long in the bathroom getting ready, keen to be as clean as possible for my big reveal. From my scalp to my toes, I was meticulously, absolutely clean, scoured outside and in. Everything other than my stinky dick of course. My shampooed and conditioned hair was done up stylishly in a manbun, a rare sight outside of work. I ran my tongue over teeth I'd already brushed twice. *Should I...?* No. Enough with the OCD. The amount of effort I'd gone too was absurd, but it felt appropriate for some reason. I mean, this would be my first time getting fully naked in front of someone in a sexual situation. Jockey could label it as a dare all he liked but it didn't change the fact I was going to be strapped naked to a chair while he watched me have multiple orgasms.

I'd even gone to the trouble of buying a new pair of Calvins for the occasion. They were ultra-white and I hoped they would make me look more tanned than what I actually was when the time came to get undressed. Accompanying my fancy briefs was a pair of slim-cut jeans, a blood-red collared shirt, dress socks, and black Vans. Just for a laugh I had even tied a pink ribbon around my caged cock. I was the present after all.

I peeked inside my jeans to inspect the ribbon was still attached when the flinging open of the front door made me jump.

Gavin came in on a gusting flurry of rain, windswept and drenched. "God, it's pissing down out there," he said, ruffling his dark hair and sending fat drops flying.

"You look like a drowned rat."

"Tell me about it. And that's just coming in from where I parked the car."

"How was Trent?"

"He was good. Donna fixed us a feed of mussels and paua so I don't need to worry about fixing myself any dinn—" Gavin's sentence ended abruptly when he finally looked over at me sat on the couch. "Phwoar! Who let the stud out, Mikey?"

A light blush tinted my cheeks.

Smiling, Gavin added, "It's a good thing I ain't a turd burglar because yours would be at serious risk of being stolen right now."

"A good old-fashioned *you look nice* would have sufficed."

"But you look better than nice." A faint smirk tugged his lips. "So who is she? What's her name?"

"It's not a date. It's Jockey's birthday."

"It is? Oh, tell him happy birthday from me." Gavin demonstrated just how classy he was when he grabbed the tea towel hanging up to dry his hair. "What bar are you boys hitting tonight?"

"I don't know. It's up to Jockey, I guess."

"Maybe I could come join you likely lads and show you how to party properly."

I knew he was joking so I replied with, "Soz, but most clubs turn pensioners away at the door these days."

"Truth be told, I'm too fucking knackered to go out tonight. I'll probably have a quiet night in and let my dentures soak in a glass of water."

I laughed. "Sounds like fun."

"Fiona's busy. Which is probably a good thing cos my balls need some rest and recuperation."

"TMI, dude."

"Anyway, it means you can borrow my car if you want, but only if you're not planning on driving drunk."

"I'm not an idiot."

Gavin raised an eye brow.

"I'm not," I insisted.

"Good. Because if you have a crash and end up a tetraplegic I don't plan on wiping your ass."

"Right back at ya."

My phone chimed with an incoming text. I swung my legs down and grabbed it off the coffee table.

Jockey: It's all set up. Ready when you are.

My cock twitched, and I went and used the small mirror near the ranch slider to give myself one last check. Gavin started laughing when he saw me slick fingers through my hair and pouting slightly at my reflection. "Are you sure you're not going on a date? Cos ya fussing like a bloody woman over there."

"It's a twenty-first. I've gotta be presentable."

"Like it matters. If it goes anything like most twenty-firsts do then half of ya there will fall asleep covered in your own vomit." He then shot me a stern look. "No driving drunk."

Rolling my eyes, I went over and asked for the car keys. My palms were sweaty, my dick still twitching. Just as I was about to leave Gavin called out to me to come back.

"Yeah?" I stared at him impatiently.

"Make sure you wear a johnny."

I screwed my face. "What are you on about now?"

"You know what I'm on about. Even if all this"—he paused to point a circling finger in my direction—"isn't for a date, there's no way in hell you're not scoring tonight looking that fucking good.

Trust me. My spidey senses know these things. Now go get 'em tiger."

I laughed. "You and your spidey sense are so fucking cringe."

He responded with a cheesy smile and a thumb up.

With a mixture of fear and savage excitement, I fetched my jacket and rushed outside to jump in the car.

Chapter 10

JOCKEY ANSWERED THE door dressed head to toe in army gear. Most days he restricted it to one item, but not tonight. The birthday boy was living his desert war fantasy in the thorn-coloured ensemble he had on. The dipshit even wore a helmet, and dog tags hung from around his neck. But it was his birthday and he could play little soldier if he wanted to.

Jockey raised his brows and grinned. I had to stifle a laugh. He'd all but started rubbing his hands together in anticipation. "You dressed up." He gave me a long, slow glance up and down. "Seriously. I reckon this is the hottest I've ever seen you look."

"Aww shucks," I replied teasingly. "These old rags were just lying around."

My funny bone died on the spot though when upon entering the sleepout I saw what was waiting for me. A black PVC sheet covered the chair he had made, cuffs attached to the arm rests and feet of the chair. On a table beside the chair was a machine that looked deathly, wires curling like snakes and several tubes that looked like they belonged in a science lab.

"Fuck. It looks like I'm about to be electrocuted."

"Ain't it cool."

"I was thinking more along the lines of fucking terrifying." I turned to hand him the tinny I'd scored for him. "Happy birthday."

"Thanks, mate."

"Is this from your mum's old dealer?"

"It is."

"Nice." Jockey eyed the cylinder-shaped foil in his hand. "His weed is the best. You should tell him to start letting me buy from him."

That was out of the question. Max Mackey—Mum's former dealer and one-time lover from before I was even born—only grew for his personal use these days. He made an exception for me because I suspect he was still madly in love with my mother.

"What do you want to drink?" Jockey asked. "I've got plenty of options."

"You choose."

He strolled to the kitchenette and fixed us both a drink, vodka and orange juice. Handing me my drink, he invited me to take a seat on the old armchair while he went and sat on the couch opposite and proceeded to just stare at me. My face grew hot under his gaze, and I cleared my throat. I took a swallow of vodka and felt it drop through my gullet in an icy burn.

"Seriously, dog. You look so frickin' handsome tonight. I didn't realise you scrubbed up so well."

"Thanks." I quickly tacked on, "you look nice too" to be polite.

My butterflies fluttered themselves out as the conversation began to flow, Jockey telling me how he'd spent the day with his brothers and aunt and uncle. It seemed sad to think his twenty-first birthday party had been a daytime affair with just his immediate family and a couple of his uncle's drinking buddies. But I was here to make up for it, which meant braving that spooky fucking chair and its menacing counterparts.

Just as we finished our drinks, Jockey stretched his arms above his head, the sinews in his neck standing out like hawsers, then shook himself loose with a pleasurable shudder. When he settled back, he was holding a small key between two fingers. It must have been under the pillow. "You know," he drawled, "I really think it's time we got this show on the road."

My heart was thumping hard enough to fracture my rib cage, but somehow I managed to get the words out. "You're the boss."

He licked his lips and glanced around the sleepout, suddenly seeming a little unsure of himself and hesitant about talking. But when his gaze returned to mine his aura of cockiness reignited. "I want you to start by taking off your shirt."

I did as he requested and draped my shirt over my shoulder.

He walked over to where I was sitting and brushed a hand across my forehead. Touching my face, his thumb grazed my bottom lip, like he was inspecting his personal property. He lifted my chin so we were looking at each other again. "Thanks for doing this for me," he whispered, then flicked the shirt off my shoulder and onto the floor. "I really appreciate it."

I blew out a breath and Jockey ran his hand down my neck, making his way to my left nipple which he tweaked with a small pinch. I winced but said nothing.

"Stand up, private," he instructed as he went to the door and locked it.

My brow skewed in confusion. Was this going to be some sort of roleplay? In a weird way that made me feel a bit better, like it was more of a game than something purely sexual.

"I told you to stand up, private," Jockey said, sterner this time.

"Yes, sir." I rose to my feet.

"Take your pants off, Freeman. And no funny business."

With a mock salute, I slid my jeans down to my knees.

"All the way, private, all the way. Lose the shoes and socks too."

I bent over and pulled my jeans off after toeing my Vans aside. My socks came off next, leaving me just my tighty-whities. The cool air of the room licked at my skin, prickling the hair on my arms. For a moment, maybe just a split-second, I almost didn't recognise the young man dressed in an army uniform standing right in front of me. His aura was so commanding. So dominant. So different to the dopey stoner I called a friend.

Staring at my bulge, Jockey pursed his lips, nodding slowly. "Now ditch those pretty knickers, private. I want to just how much of a man you are."

I shucked the Calvins down and watched him smile as he caught sight of the ribbon. It forced him to break character and he chuckled. "That's a nice touch. Nice touch indeed."

"Happy birthday." I smiled back. "Maybe you'd like to unwrap your present now?"

Jockey shook his head, reverting back to the army fantasy. "All in good time, private. We need to carry out an inspection first."

"An inspection?"

"Silence," he snapped. "Just stand at attention, Freeman. Arms at your sides. Let me get a good look at you."

Reluctantly, I rest my arms at my side. I'd never been so exposed before, not like this. I was almost grateful to be wearing the chastity device because at least it offered some sort of barrier between Jockey and my full nudity.

He stepped closer, gaze aimed at my enclosed dick that suddenly felt miniscule inside its tiny cage. Jockey began to circle me, his dark eyes burning into my naked flesh. I started shivering when he came to a stop behind me, his hand groping my ass.

"Mmm. That's a nice ass you got there, Freeman. I bet you're popular with the boys back in the barracks."

I could hardly hear above the pounding of the blood in my temples. My mouth was dry, lips heavy. "Yeah," I exhaled nervously.

"I bet they'd all love to have a go on this." He gave my ass a good slap, making me jump. "It's too bad that's not a pussy between your legs. Otherwise I'd be tempted to have a go on this sweet ass of yours."

Was this a joke? Part of the fantasy? I was about to call time on this stunt of his when Jockey suddenly appeared in front of me, his hands making quick work of the ribbon which he let float to the floor.

Knowing I was seconds away from freedom calmed me down, or maybe it was just that my dick's lust for freedom outweighed any anxiety.

"Those balls of yours look pretty full, private. You been brewing up a big load for me, have you?"

"Yes, sir. The biggest."

I let out a small squeak when his hand made a sudden move for my balls, squeezing them gently and commanding me to cough.

I did so, weakly.

"Cough again. A man's cough. Not a bitch cough."

I coughed more fully this time, my balls bouncing in the heat of his sweaty palm. I didn't like him touching me like this. That hadn't been part of the deal. But I said nothing, deciding it was better to give my friend the birthday present he had asked for.

His fingers rubbed the smooth texture of my nut sac. "When did you last shave your balls, private?"

"This evening, sir."

"And why was that?"

I hesitated. "Because I wanted to be presentable for you, sir. For your birthday."

I could tell he was trying not to smile. Jockey's hand remained glued to my nuts, frisky fingers exploring the smooth orbs of my testicles. I couldn't help but wonder what Brian would make of this. There would be no way he would have let Jockey take a dare this far. No fucking way. I imagined Brian standing here with us, cussing me out for being such a homo.

My face began to burn with shame when Jockey's touching became sensual and my dick tried to harden inside its cage. I willed it to go down but it refused, struggling to inflate to its full potential. Eventually the swelling became painful and I sucked back a hiss.

"What's wrong, private?" Jockey asked, still playing with my balls.

"My dick, sir. It hurts."

"Why is it hurting, Freeman?"

Fucker. He was going to make me say it. "Because it's trying to get hard, sir."

"Are you a poofter or something? Can't you let a man touch your balls without getting turned on?"

I scowled, letting him know he was crossing a line.

Jockey smiled and let go, clearly getting the hint. Taking a step back, he began to pace back and forth in front of me, hands laced behind his back. "It has been brought to my attention that you have broken protocol and ventured out of the base without permission. Is this true?"

I wondered where he was going with this but I played along, grateful to not have his hand locked on my balls anymore. "Yes, sir, but I had a very good reason."

"And what reason is that, Freeman?"

"I was hungry and needed to buy a Big Mac."

An intrigued half smile on his face. "There's no McDonalds in the desert."

"Yeah there is. It's round the corner from my mate's house."

"Is that so?" He stopped pacing, turning to face me and look me over some more. "And did you buy this Big Mac before or after you ass raped Alice the camel and her daughter?"

My mouth farted out a giggle. Trust Jockey to inject some feral humour into something like this.

"This isn't a laughing matter, private. Unless these camels gave you permission to be ass raped then we have a problem."

Smirking, I replied. "They gave me their full permission, sir. Alice the camel let me hump all her humps."

"That might be the case with Alice, she's a slut, but her underage daughter is a good girl who would not let vermin like you near her virginal camel toe."

"Nar, she was a filthy slag just like her mother."

"Enough!" He raised a hand like he was about to strike me. "Now, we have a way to punish and cure you of this deviousness. So if you would please take a seat."

That wiped the smile off my face. I turned to look at the chair, my stomach twisting into knots.

"What are you waiting for, Freeman? The throne is yours."

"Are you going to unlock me first, sir? Before I sit down?"

He pretended to think it over before saying, "I suppose that would be a good idea." Stepping forward, he slipped the key into the padlock and turned the key and the most glorious *click* sounded. With great care, he freed my balls and removed the cage.

"Thank fuck for that," I sighed.

"Feel good to be free does it?"

"You bet."

"The poor little guy looks a little messy," Jockey said as he stroked my dick. "And he looks a little fucking stinky."

"That happens if you can't wash your cock for five days."

"You can take a shower after we've done. Sound good?"

I nodded.

Clearly whatever the roleplay was before had come to an end. Now it was time to get down to business. And that business saw me reluctantly approach the chair to be strapped in for the next two hours. He'd promised me to turn the machine off if I needed a break from being milked, but being my ass being cuffed to the chair for two hours was non-negotiable.

Jockey got down on one knee and proceeded to restrain me. He started with my hands, clipping them into the cuffs on the armrest before locking my feet to the legs of the chair. A small tug at the restraints told me they were secure and there was no escape. My ass was locked in if I liked it or not.

He removed his helmet and got to work on hooking me up to the machine. Every step of the way he was gentle, caring even, wanting to make sure I was comfortable. When it came time to put the tube on, he played with my dick and said, "I'm just going to give it a little suck so you're hard enough for the tube to stay on."

"It really needs a wash first."

"A little mess don't scare me." And on those words he dipped his head and took my grateful cock inside his mouth.

It was just a little suck, like he'd said, more maintenance than for any enjoyment. He didn't have to suck it for long, my dick had missed his lips and was well past semi in no time.

"I think someone is ready for the best night of his life," Jockey said, giving the tip of my cock one last sticky kiss.

"Of your life more like it," I replied feebly. "I'm only doing this for you, remember?"

My comment didn't get a response.

Jockey stood up and went to examine the machine and equipment resting on the nearby table. He was locked in concentration, playing with dials, examining the tubes. "These come in three different sizes," he explained to me, pointing to the three tubes on the table. He craned his neck to study my penis for a moment and said, "I think we'll go with the medium for you."

"Cool." I harumphed. "At least it's not the small size."

"There is no small. Just medium, large, and extra-large."

"Oh." I wanted to believe that meant the underhung were out of luck but I knew that probably wasn't the case. My dick just happened to belong to the same tribe of modest.

Jockey slathered my eager cock with lube and proceeded to fit me into the tube, which he called the milking sleeve. It slipped off the first couple of times but eventually he got it so it was secure.

He stood off to the side, fiddling with the machine some more. He then disappeared behind me and I assumed it was to plug something in but instead it was to slip a ball gag in my mouth.

I started shaking my head, trying to free my hands so I could pull it out, which of course I couldn't. "We didn't agree to me being gagged" is what I tried to say but it came out more like "Vree bdnt mgre ru vis."

"Calm down, dog. It's all part of the fun. If I don't gag you then you'll make too much noise, and I don't fancy my uncle coming out here to see what we're up to."

I stopped struggling but my eyes were wide with fury. I didn't like surprises, and I didn't like being tricked.

"You're all good, bro. You're in safe hands." He stroked my chest. "You know I'd never do anything to hurt you."

Easy for him to say. He wasn't the one strapped to a fucking chair about to have his cock raped by a machine.

"And don't worry. The second I see any blood I'll turn it off."

Blood! I moaned through the gag, my feet and hands shaking to break free. But Jockey ignored my protests and returned to the machine. I sat there a bundle of nerves, like an inmate waiting for the executioner to flick the switch. And then he did and my eyes rolled to the back of my head and I let out the softest of pleasurable groans.

"Yeah," Jockey said. "It feels good, doesn't it?"

I moaned some more, nodding deliriously.

"I told you you'd enjoy this. Now I'm gonna sit back and listen to your pretty noises and wait for that first cup of cum."

I don't know how pretty I sounded but I was certainly making lots of noise; moans, groans and croaky squeaks. It felt amazing. While I shivered in ecstasy, the gag left me drooling down my chin and onto my chest. But I didn't care, I was too focused on the magic happening to my cock.

Jockey shifted the armchair over so that he was sat directly in front of me. He sat back and enjoyed his drink while he watched the pump abuse my cock. I noticed he had a remote with him which I assumed meant he could control the speed from the comfort of his chair. "Now this is what I call a birthday party," he said, using the remote to increase the speed a little.

It didn't take long for him to get the first orgasm out of me, my long high-pitched groan letting him know I'd just ejaculated. The machine slowed to a stop.

Grinning like he had canary feathers stuck in his teeth, Jockey came over and unhooked a cup from the end of the tube that had sucked the cum out of my balls. He held the cup up to the light, admiring the creamy contents. "Damn, private... Look how much cum is in this thing. You must have been busting to let that one out." He tipped the cup up and drizzled the ropey white river of cum into his mouth. "Mmm. Tasty."

There wasn't a chance for me to be shocked because he immediately reapplied the cup to the tube and switched the machine back on. Once again I was moaning behind the ball gag, my bare ass writhing in the PVC-clad seat. This time was more uncomfortable because I'd just lost my lollies but somehow the machine managed to suck me to a full erection again and within minutes I was drained of a second load.

Once again, Jockey removed the cum cup and drank my sexual essence and licked his lips after letting out a semen-flavoured burp. This time he allowed me a break and switched the machine off. That was when I felt most awkward. Without the orgasmic bliss tickling my balls, I had nothing to do but sit there and watch him watch me.

He lit a cigarette. The paper at the end crackled as he sucked a deep draught of smoke into his lungs. Staring at my tube-covered cock, he let the smoke back out. I followed his gaze as it dipped to my feet and slowly climbed up my body, like he was mapping every inch into his memory to use at a later date.

Minutes ticked by incredibly slowly. Finally, Jockey was ready to resume my milking. He switched the machine back on and I was positive I had no more milk to give. But like a crowded high-rise elevator stopping at every single floor on the punctuated journey to the ground level, I eased up by degrees and eventually got off again. Once again I was left a panting mess, sweat now dripping down my brow and chest, my inner thighs moist from all my squirming. I waited for my mock sergeant to switch off the machine, empty the cup, and allow me a short break to recuperate.

But that didn't happen this time.

Suddenly, what had been a steady pace thundered into full gallop as Jockey turned the dial in his hands. The milk sleeve refused to let my exhausted cock deflate. There was still some of the bliss but now it was mingled pain. Heaven and hell were wrapped around my penis, and I was constantly battling to know which one I was enduring. It was torture, the strangest torture I had ever experienced. I almost wished for some blood to appear so he would turn the damn thing off, but then my dick would tingle in that special way and I'd find myself trying to lift my hips to return the tube fuck-pumps of my own.

But following each brief foray into bliss was a dark dive back to the depths of agony. A twisted agony that grew in intensity the longer my dick got raped by the tube.

"VROCKY! FRURN IDT FROTH! FURN ID OFF!"

My pleading screams went unanswered and I gave up trying to form words, my voice instead morphing into mewling howls like some sort of wild animal. I was unable to sit still but also unable to get away. My eyes were blinking furiously, trying to communicate to Jockey that he needed to turn the machine off immediately. But he didn't.

Jockey just sat back, rested a languid ankle on his knee, carrying on drinking and chain-smoking like my ordeal was a source of entertainment.

"MMMRRPHH! MMMRRPPHH! AWWRRR!" my wild cries continued.

By this point I was delirious, not even taking notice of my cruel master sitting a few feet away. I could have been plonked in the middle of Times Square and not known. Every so often I would unleash a girly squawk, an orgasmic cry if you will, as my balls were forced to climax against their will. Each climax contained that familiar squiggly zap along my taint, the pleasure of release, but now when my semen shot out my dick it was accompanied with stinging pain. By now I was only ejaculating watery trickles, much like I used to shoot in the days before my balls had properly dropped. In fact, I was pretty sure some of what I was leaking was piss but I couldn't be sure. All I knew was that I had been strapped to the chair a horned-up man but had been reduced to a blubbering little boy.

Just when I thought I'd reached my final limit, past the five other final limits I'd already passed, the machine made a loud beep and the tube slowed to a stop.

Panting heavily, I looked over to see Jockey getting to his feet. "Well done, private," he said. "That was an amazing effort. I think I counted four loads during that round."

With a confident smirk and cocky stroll, he came and stood right in front of me. Rather than remove the tube and feast on the sperm I'd been robbed of, he then ran his thumb over the angle of my jaw and smiled, wolf eyes gleaming. "Before I let you go, Mike, there's something I've been dying to do to you for a while now."

My panic at his statement quickly alleviated when he sat down on the floor and uncuffed my feet. Was he letting me go after all? Had his comment been a joke?

Looking at me, Jockey slowly raised my right foot and caressed it, his hand warm and strong. He watched my face carefully, then said directly to me, "You have such sexy feet."

I what now?

He gently encompassed my foot with his fingers and praised its symmetry, its supposed gracefulness. With a sultry look in his dark eyes, magnetic like a predator, he inspected my foot even closer, letting his earnest appreciation speak for itself. Jockey breathed one more word of praise, "Beautiful." Then, raising it slightly higher to his mouth, he kissed the arch tenderly. He ran his thumb across the arch and sole and turned it somewhat, before kissing it again.

I gasped behind the ball gag.

Training his gaze on me, Jockey continued to caress my foot, toes, and ankle tenderly. He spread kisses along the upper curve of the arch and to the tops of my toes, then dragging his mouth along the top of my foot; he kissed hard the pulse at my ankle. My heart raced madly; I knew he could feel it. Slowly, he lowered my foot back to the floor.

Then it was my other foot's turn. It too was clasped, caressed, kissed and licked. By the time he was finished showering it with affection, once again telling me how "beautiful" my feet were, my foot was covered with a sheen of his saliva.

He rose up on his knees and removed the ball gag, his face inches from mine. Was he about to kiss me? I was so fucking dizzy I didn't know what was happening. Instead, he whispered in my ear, "I believe your two hours are up, private" and proceeded to unhook me from the machine.

Chapter 11

PARKED BENEATH A GIANT palm tree down near the beach, I stared out at the darkness of the Pacific Ocean. Nursing a beer in my hand, I inhaled the pungent pot smoke clogging the air in Gavin's shitbox Honda Civic. Following my quick shower after being drained of every ounce of cum in my body, Jockey had suggested we continue celebrating his birthday "Lana Del Ray styles" and get high by the beach. I'd gladly gone along with the suggestion, keen to get out of his sleepout and not lay eyes on that ghastly milk machine ever again.

"Fuck, man," came from the passenger seat, the words croaked around escaping wisps of smoke.

Turning my head, I watched Jockey let the rest of the smoke drift lazily from his open mouth.

"It's pretty fucking good," Jockey said of the pot. "Pretty fucking good indeed."

"So it gets the birthday boy's seal of approval?"

"You know it." He turned and smiled. "But maybe next year you can shout me a trip to the whore house instead."

"When a hooker's rates are as cheap as the green your puffing then I'll be sure to do that."

That earned a snigger from Jockey as I took another sip on my drink. I stared back out to sea, wondering what Brian was up to. It was weird him not being here tonight. Birthdays were always a party of three but from now on they would only be a party of two—just me and Jockey. *Me, Jockey and his secret fetish for my feet.*

Well, I guess it wasn't all that secret anymore.

It had been nearly two hours since leaving his sleepout, and so far we'd both kept our promise to not talk about the dare. That's what I had wanted. Just to do it and forget it. And for the most part I did want to forget it, but I also had questions. They were whizzing about in my head, dragged to the surface of my mind from some of what Jockey had done and said earlier.

Finished with the joint, Jockey put it out in the car's ashtray, leaned back in his seat and laced his hands over his stomach. He looked so relaxed, so unbothered by the events that had taken place inside his sleepout.

"Are you queer?" The words popped out of me like a blender losing its lid.

There was a long silence. Jockey turned his head, squinting open one eye. I thought I should say something more, but didn't know what.

Breaking the quiet, Jockey said, "Some might say I'm very odd."

"I don't mean queer like that. I mean, do you like getting off with other guys?"

"There's one guy whose dick I suck every Friday night. You might know him. I think we both have a lot of fun."

"I'm being serious. Have you hooked up with other guys?"

Another span of silence before Jockey's voice came back: "A couple."

"A couple?"

"Five others to be exact."

I laughed, although there was nothing funny about what he'd said. "Are you cruising Hickford Park or something?"

"Fuck no. Nothing like that. I don't go looking for it." Jockey sighed when he saw my face still riddled with questions. "When I was dating Fiona she liked to bring other guys into the bedroom. Said she liked a bit of man on man action and I pride myself on pleasing my woman. Any way I can."

"She wanted to watch you with other men?"

"Yeah. She was into it in a big way."

"So what exactly did you do with these guys? That's if you don't mind me asking."

"We'd usually take turns fucking Fiona and then suck each other off."

"Wow..."

"Yeah. It was actually pretty hot. You know the saying 'a spoonful of sugar makes the medicine go down'? Well, I can assure you that a nice layer of pussy juice makes the cock go down just as good."

I knew he'd said that to try and get a laugh out of me, but I was too dumbstruck for humour right now. None of this should have come as a shock, yet somehow it did.

"Is that all you did? Just suck dick?"

"I fucked two of the guys," he said like it was no big deal. "The others weren't as keen to go that far."

"You fucked them? You actually put your dick in their ass?"

"That's usually how fucking a dude goes, Mike." Jockey sniggered. "You stick it up their shitter, not their earhole."

"I know but..." I shook my head. "And you liked it?"

"My dick likes any tight hole, and an asshole can be pretty fucking tight." He chuckled arrogantly, knowingly. "And I gotta say there is something hot about nailing a bloke. Makes ya feel more dominant. More like an alpha. Like a victorious soldier."

I wasn't surprised to hear him liken sex to war, but I sure as fuck was surprised by the rest of this conversation. I felt weird, really weird to be honest, but I was also sort of jealous to discover Jockey was much more sexually experienced than I'd ever assumed.

"Did you let any of the guys fuck you?"

"Never." His response was swift and adamant. "My asshole is a one-way street. No fucker is cornholing me."

Why did that answer annoy me so much? I shouldn't have cared what his sexual preferences were with other men.

"I can't believe you never told me any of this before."

"Here's the guts of it, Mike," Jockey said bluntly. "If I had told you any of this you would have run off and gabbed about it to Brian, who we both know would be an utter prick about it. There's also the fact that what Fiona and I did together in private is no one's business but ours. We don't owe you or anyone an explanation."

"I know—"

"And lastly, you get super fucking weird if I bring up anything too sexual. You always have."

"No I don't."

"You fucking do, bro. I've been sucking you off for how long now? And we still never really talk about it. The few times I have tried to bring it up you go all weird on me. It's a miracle tonight even happened."

"Maybe I'm just a private person."

"Or maybe you need to pull the stick out of your ass. You need to relax, man. Sex ain't a big deal."

"It sort of is when you're still a virgin."

"I've told you what to do to solve that problem. Go to the—"

"Whore parlour. I know."

"Why don't you?"

"Because the thought of paying someone for sex doesn't float my boat."

"Trust me, dog, once you're balls deep in that pussy it will float your boat big time." He then narrowed his eyes. "Or a bloke's hairy asshole if that's more to your liking."

A lingering silence filled the vehicle as I tried to absorb everything Jockey had just shared. A part of me wanted to change topics and talk about something else but a bigger part of me needed some clarity.

Gathering my courage, I asked, "So you've sucked five dicks but still consider yourself straight?"

"Six dicks," he corrected. "You forgot to include yours. The sexiest one of all."

"That just proves the point even more, doesn't it? You're not straight."

"Does it matter?" he answered accusingly, making me feel like a bigot.

"N-Nar, man," I stuttered, quick to back off. "Not at all. I don't care who you sleep with."

"Good. Because I'm still the same dopey fucker you've been mates with all these years. Where I put my dick shouldn't change any of that."

"You're right. I'm sorry."

"'S okay. I know it must come as a bit of a shock to find out the guy who sucks you off every Friday night isn't one hundred percent straight."

"Don't rub it in." I gave him a playful nudge with my elbow. "I'm embarrassed enough as it is."

"Don't be embarrassed. I think it's kinda cute. I love how innocent you are. It just makes me wanna corrupt you even more."

"I don't think I want a cock-monger corrupting me, thanks."

"A cock-monger." He threw his head back and laughed. "I like that."

It went quiet again as Jockey sparked up a cigarette, only the lapping waves sounding off. Jockey was lucky I'd been drinking or there was no way I'd have handled this conversation so casually. Because if there was one thing that was true from everything he'd said tonight, it was that I was certainly guilty of having a stick up my ass sometimes.

That made me wonder if the pretend soldier sat beside me had done me a favour tonight; pushing me outside of my comfort zone. I hadn't enjoyed the pain I'd endured—my dick feeling like it'd been sucked within an inch of its life—but I had already decided the orgasmic bliss had outweighed all that. And maybe finding out he had a thing for my feet wasn't a bad thing either. Kinda fucking weird, sure, but not bad. It meant Jockey was comfortable with me, and that could only be a good thing.

"Not to be crude," Jockey said, stretching his legs as much as the car allowed, "but my dick is so fucking hard right now."

Out of the corner of my eye, I could see him running the palm of his hand across his crotch, the cigarette clamped between two fingers. He brought it to his mouth and took another drag while he rolled down the window a crack or two with his other hand. Out the butt went.

"What about you?" he asked. "Are you hard?"

"Your machine has left me limp as a soggy biscuit."

"Do you wanna be?"

"Hard?"

"Yeah. I reckon my mouth can resurrect little Mikey down there no sweat. Now that you've had them balls of yours emptied so thoroughly you can sit back and enjoy without worrying about nutting too soon."

"But it's not Friday."

Jockey laughed. "Your dick doesn't know what day it is."

As I stole another look at Jockey's crotch, he stirred restlessly, eyes turned toward the darkness beyond the passenger window. It wasn't like I didn't want a blowjob, that would be like turning down free money, but I didn't want us to make this a habit that happened more than once a week.

But it is his birthday...

"Okay." I widened my legs and pointed down towards my dick. "Happy birthday."

He reached over to undo my jeans and pull the zipper down, then slid his hand inside. I closed my eyes as Jockey's fingers found my cock and squeezed the head gently. My dick reacted positively to his touch, stiffening and lengthening within his grip.

"Nice," he whispered in my ear, his breath hot on my neck. "I love playing with your dick. It's the perfect size for my hand. Not too big and not too small."

"Thanks...I think?"

"It's a compliment. Your dick is sexy, just like you."

"But is it as sexy as my feet?" I said, flashing him a piss-taking grin.

He laughed, his hand still groping, still arousing. "I thought you might find a way to bring that up."

"It doesn't freak me out if that's what you think."

"Are you sure?"

"I actually sort of liked how you sucked my toes. Felt good. I'd let you do it again if you wanted to."

"Would you now?" He stroked the tip of my cock with his thumb, making me shudder. "Maybe we need to incorporate some toe sucking into our Friday night fun?"

"Yeah."

"And maybe you could start turning up wearing different sorts of clothes."

"I thought you liked what I was wearing tonight?"

"I do, but you always wear jeans. Even in summer. It'd be nice if you wore a pair of shorts for once." His hand dipped lower and groped my balls. "You've got nice legs, Mike, and you should show them off more."

Eyes still closed. "Should I?"

"Fucking oath you should." He gave my balls a light squeeze. "They're nice and toned and the right amount of hairy."

"What's the right amount of hairy?"

"Enough to be seen but not hairy like a forest."

"You mean like yours," I teased as I opened my eyes.

"Mine aren't like a forest." Maintaining his grip on my junk, he used his other hand to pull up the leg of his pants, flashing a hint of hairy shin. "That's just normal hairy."

"They're pretty fucking hair, bro."

"Maybe you're right," he conceded and dropped the pant leg down. "But my point is you have nice legs and you'd be doing the world a favour if you showed them off more."

"I'll keep that in mind."

I closed my eyes again and let myself enjoy the touch of his hand and the slow massage of my balls. I was also enjoying having my ego rubbed. He'd never told me these things before and I gotta say I was lapping it up. So much so I asked him, "What else about me do you like?"

"All of you is hot but if I had to pick one thing then I'd have to say your ass. Some days when you turn up in jeans that are a little tighter than normal I bust a woody on the spot. It looks so fuckable."

Not as fuckable as yours, I thought.

"If you were up for it I could make you feel real good if you let me explore the backdoor one night. Mmm."

"You're not fucking my ass, Jockey," I said, deadpan.

I gasped as his hand opened again and again, holding both my dick and balls hostage. Jockey fondled my flesh in his grip, my balls bulging between his fingers and my pulsating dick twitching in his palm. I could only stare back at him in awe of what was happening. He pumped me slowly, his fingers gripping me tightly. I swallowed hard. I wasn't sure I could hold out much longer.

"I'm gonna come if you keep doing that," I told him softly.

Jockey stopped what he was doing. Giving the head of my dick a final squeeze, he removed his hand and brought it back to his own lap. Lifting it to his lips, he inserted a finger into his mouth and licked my wetness from his skin.

Then he cupped his palm around his nose and inhaled.

"Your balls smell great," he said. "How about we go down to the beach so I can give them a good lick."

"Why can't you lick them here?"

"Because the steering wheel is in the way. I don't wanna get a concussion if you start fucking my face like you normally do."

"Fair point."

"I was also thinking it might be nice for the birthday boy to suck you off while you're in just your birthday suit."

"Haven't you seen me naked enough for one night?"

"Are you kidding? I could never get enough of seeing you naked."

"I bet you say that to all the boys," I joked.

"Come on, bro. It's my birthday," he whined, his voice becoming an octave higher and petulant. "I'm not asking you to do anything in return. Just lay down naked and let me suck that sexy dick of yours."

"What if there are people down there?"

"It's after midnight. The only ones here are us."

I stared out at the beach, the sandy strip looked deserted. "Fine," I relented, "but only because it's your birthday."

"Thanks, man. You're the best."

I had assumed we would make our way down to the beach right away but instead Jockey grabbed us each a beer from the backseat. "Here," he said, passing me the can. "I think we'll both enjoy it more after another beer."

"But I'm driving. I've already had too much to drink."

"Live a little."

"We'll live longer if I don't drive us home drunk."

"Come on. It's just one more beer, and I think you're gonna need it."

"Why will I need it?" I asked, feeling worried.

"So you've got something to wash down all the compliments I'm about to give you when I see you naked."

"In that case, I guess one more beer won't hurt." I tore the tab off the can and guzzled back a mouthful of beer, inwardly cursing myself for my ego's weakness. And for being such a fucking, fucking idiot.

Chapter 12

AN HOUR LATER, WE FINALLY exited the vehicle and made our way down to the beach. That one extra beer Jockey had suggested had somehow turned into three. In the back of my mind was the not-so small worry about how the fuck I was supposed to drive us home now that I was undoubtedly over the limit. I figured I could call Gavin if I absolutely had to, but I'd rather avoid costing him a taxi fare—and avoid the lecture that would follow—just so he could come and drive us home.

The sandy stretch of coast was deserted just like Jockey said it would be. The privacy of our surroundings calmed me somewhat, although I still questioned why on earth I'd agreed to give him an extra birthday present. The dare with the milking machine should have been enough. But something—there was something that just rendered me utterly irrational, like I was back in middle school and falling victim to my raging hormones all over again. But, in all honesty, did anyone ever really grow out of that?

We walked for about a hundred yards when Jockey suddenly stepped in front of me and spun around, placing both his hands on my shoulders. He stared back at me for what felt like ages, his eyes scanning my face and taking in my appearance. I returned his seeking gaze and allowed myself the chance to really look at him without feeling at all self-conscious.

"You are so fucking handsome, Mike. Seriously, bro. You're the best-looking dude in town in my books."

"You're just saying that cos your drunk and horny." The bubble of laughter in my voice held no mockery, merely a hint of the pleasure I took in Jockey's mischievous flirtation.

"Ain't gonna lie. I'm certainly both those things right now but that doesn't mean it isn't true. I've always had a thing for you."

"A thing for me?"

"You know...a crush."

"Blimey. All your secrets are coming out tonight."

"I don't have secrets," he said. "Just things I haven't shared with you yet."

I began to feel woozy while butterflies made themselves at home in my tummy. His grip on my shoulders was making me weak as the heat from his palms penetrated my shirt and I could tell he wanted to kiss me. I felt his hand sneak its way to my neck where he applied pressure, bringing my face down to his waiting lips.

I moaned against him as his tongue passed through my lips and into my mouth, feverishly pressing against my own. Within seconds I was nothing but sensation. My head was spinning as I slowly took in what was happening; *I'm kissing Jockey Savage! I'm kissing Jockey and I'm enjoying it!*

I let my head fall back, exposing my neck to him and Jockey took it as his cue to begin to work on it. Wet butterfly kisses covered my throat and traced the contours of my collar bone making my moans deepen as my skin became alive at the sensation of his stubble scraping against it. I dropped my arms limply at my sides as Jockey sank slowly to his knees, his hands trailing behind and worshipping at my chest as he travelled down my body.

Hungrily he lifted my shirt and let his tongue marvel all over my stomach. The feeling of his wet mouth licking my stomach made my knees buckle. I could already tell his tongue was experienced as it lapped over my tummy and traced the trail of fine hairs that disappeared down into my jeans.

"Fuck, I want you so badly," he moaned into the night air as he began unbuckling my belt. His fingers made clumsy work of it, desire causing him to struggle. He looked up at me through half-lidded eyes, "Take off your shirt."

Half-numb from a breakdown in my ability to continue processing this situation, I stared dumbly at my friend. I knew I'd agreed to get naked for him but between the kissing and his confession about a crush, I wondered just how far this was going to go.

"Take your shirt off," he repeated.

I did as I was told, unbuttoning my shirt and letting it slip from my body and onto the sand below. Jockey looked up at my naked chest and forgot about my belt, lifting himself enough off the ground to wrap his lips around my right nipple. I called out suddenly as the feeling of his tongue massaging my nipple made it rise and harden.

I could feel the outline of his cock pressing up against my thigh as he licked my pecs. His tongue lapped furiously at my chest, leaving the skin hot and wet as it passed over. Ignoring the voice in my head telling me to put a stop to this, my hands got in the game and quickly lifted and clawed at Jockey's army shirt, desperately trying to tear it off so my eyes could finally feast themselves on his body.

Both of us were moaning so loudly I couldn't tell who was making what sound. He pulled back for a moment and helped me remove his top. My mouth dropped as he pulled his shirt off over his head. He too stopped for a moment, letting his shirt fall to the sand beneath our feet. In the light from the voyeuristic moon, the deep colour of his tanned skin shone almost golden in the shadows. It was as if I was staring at him through new eyes, slowly realising just how toned Jockey was. He wasn't some muscle-bound hound by any means, his body still sinewy, but those biceps and pecs had more power and definition than I'd ever given him credit for.

Damn. All that manual labour you've been doing has really paid off.

My gaze studied the dark hair on his chest before settling on his slim waist and washboard stomach. His chest rose and fell with every sharp intake of breath he took, a signal that if he didn't pounce soon he might lose it right here in his pants.

He lifted his right hand and wrapped it around the back of my head, pulling me in for another a kiss. We collided so hard I was sure he cut my lip, but I didn't care. I was so overcome with a need to be close to him that I quickly finished what he had started with my belt and with his tongue still in my mouth, sucking on my own, I let my jeans fall to the ground and kicked my sneakers off in the process.

He pulled away for a second to mirror my actions. Then pausing again to take in the situation, we both looked around once again. Within seconds we were naked except for our underwear. His slim legs were well defined and covered with dark, masculine curly hairs that trailed from his thighs right down to his ankles.

There we were. Standing in just our underwear on the beach. In plain sight of anyone who dared to walk by or just happen to find themselves on the beach at such a late hour. The thrill of getting caught was making me shiver and shake. All I knew was that I wanted to feel his body against mine so badly at this point that I didn't care if we had an audience.

I trailed my eyes down to his dark pair of underwear and the generous bulge that was buried inside. I reached out and started rubbing at it, keeping my eyes focused on his to gauge his reaction. He closed his eyes, letting them roll back inside his head as I massaged his dick through the soft cotton of his boxer briefs.

"*Yessss*," he breathed, sucking air in through clenched teeth. "Keep rubbing it, baby."

It didn't dawn on me at first that he'd just called me baby. I was too entranced by my hand's worshipping of the bulge in his underwear.

"I didn't realise your dick was so big," I said—part flirt, part fact.

"It is big," he said without an ounce of modesty. "But that only makes it taste better."

I knew what he was hinting at but I ignored it, content for now to just rub it through his precum-soaked briefs.

"Go on, baby," he whispered. "Give it a try. For the birthday boy?"

"I don't know."

"I promise to make it up to you." He licked and bit my neck. "I know something that will drive you wild."

I swallowed hard. A warm feeling spread through me. I was so uncertain of myself. I wanted more time to think, or get used to the idea. But I allowed him to gently push me down until I was kneeling before him. I looked up and saw him mouth the words *please baby?* My gaze fell from his, down his fit body, landing on his bulging briefs. His cock was so close I could sense the heat oozing from his crotch.

This was uncharted territory for me. Everything was so familiar but so unusual. I knew what a dick looked like. I knew what he wanted me to do with it. But I'd never been the one in this position. I felt like a different person altogether.

Ignoring all thought, I moved in. First I pressed my lips against the shaft. Through the fabric, I could feel its shape tighten and surge back against my face. My hands rubbed at the sides of Jockey's hips while I slowly drank in the feeling of his crotch in my face. I opened my mouth and gently bit at the girth of flesh.

I couldn't wait. My fingers tugged down at Jockey's underwear. I wouldn't forget the sight of his cock being freed, bouncing stiff in front of me and pointed right at my face. Reaching up, I took it in my fingers and tipped it upward to marvel at its every feature. It was so similar to mine, yet different in so many ways. It wasn't like I'd never seen his dick before but this was the first time I'd ever had such a close and personal view of its beauty, and size.

My head moved toward the tip in a trance. I planted my lips right against the end. My tongue flicked out and teased at the slit. I opened just a little wider and took more of the head in my lips and slid back again. The third time I felt Jockey nod in my hands, his shaft swelling back against my fingers.

With each taste I grew more addicted. It only took seconds. I opened my mouth and slurped in the fat tip of Jockey's dick. I did it again. I slid further. I wanted more. His shaft slid over my tongue. It was so strange. This throbbing thing in my mouth was attached to Jockey. He was in me.

Mindlessly, I ran my hands up and down his hairy legs, clutching the firm muscles of his calves and thighs, desperate to explore the strength of his body. I closed my eyes and focused on that beautiful cock, lathering it with love and slurping praise. I couldn't take more than half inside me. His dick was just too big and my throat too inexperienced. I pulled it from my mouth and licked the entire shaft. His scent filled my nose when my mouth slurped at the hairy base of his shaft.

I reached for his balls and began fondling them. They were full and heavy, carrying stocks of arousal that had built up through our entire evening together. They demanded to be emptied. They *deserved* to be emptied.

Diving under Jockey's dick I went for those balls and took moist flesh into my mouth. I mouthed them gently while rolling one around on my wet tongue. His taste was stronger here, more musky, more manly. I was getting lost in that smell until I felt my hair getting tugged.

"That's enough for now, baby." Jockey said. "It's my turn to make you feel good."

He gathered our discarded clothes and laid them out like a blanket then guided me down to lay on my back. Standing above me, he told me to take my briefs off. I did so, leaving me every bit as naked as he was.

Jockey picked up my briefs and pressed them to his face and breathed in the smells trapped within the material. I propped myself on my elbows and looked on with my mouth gaped open.

"Fuck yeah," he growled. "I could smell these bad boys all day."

After three more sniffs, he tossed them aside and moved to the ground between my thighs. They opened for him. My cock lay bobbing back toward me, leaving it no secret that I was enjoying Jockey's birthday present just as much as he was.

Without warning, he dove onto my crotch. Unlike my amateur efforts, Jockey deepthroated my entire length on the first plunge. The moan I released was loud, as if it had been building up since the moment he'd molested my junk in the car.

Up and down. Up and down. The smooth glide of his lips was sensational as my cock tickled his tonsils on every downward plunge. I began to feel more like myself again with us both in our usual places. Him the cocksucker, me the cocksuckee. I grabbed his head, adding some force to the cocksucking rhythm.

"Suck that dick, buddy. Yeah. Suck it good."

Jockey did just that. Sucking it good. Coating me with heat and spit until I could feel a puddle of saliva gathering in my pubes.

"Now do my balls," I demanded. "Suck them."

More than happy to take an order, the birthday boy slurped his way off my cock and kissed his way down to my nuts. His stubble brushed the sensitive skin of my balls as his tongue danced between them.

Suddenly, my legs were hoisted in the air on two strong hands. His fingers and thumbs dug into my skin, though I quickly realized I loved the feeling. Deeper Jockey went, his tongue flattening itself and diving lower. My scrotum becoming a bulging mass atop Jockey's nose.

My eyes widened when I felt the flat of Jockey's tongue slide over my asshole.

"No. Don't put that in—"

My voice was lost to a whining groan as Jockey began licking up and down my hair-lined trench. My head fell back. All of me did. I lay on our makeshift blanket with my legs spread open in Jockey's hands. It was such a peculiar feeling, yet insanely erotic, quite like nothing I had ever experienced before. Jockey's tongue lapped at the rim of my asshole, wagging and digging against my most private area.

If I hadn't been lost to such overwhelming pleasure I would have been mortified to have someone's tongue licking around the part of my body I shit out of. It wasn't like I hadn't heard of rimming before but I just thought it was something porn stars did.

And Jockey apparently.

My feet twitched about in the air, my toes curling with every delicious deep lick he inflicted on me. *We are definitely adding this to the list for our Friday nights*. He could suck my dick, my balls, my toes, my ass. Hell, he could suck wherever he liked.

All at once he rose. My sack dragged down his face while his tongue slid up between my balls, up the length of my cock to the very tip. And he dove onto it again. My entire cock was buried in this horny fucker's face. My legs were let go to fall. I watched Jockey push his mouth down to the base of my dick. I tried to cry out, but when I opened my mouth, a powerful hand was at my cheek. I groaned and turned to meet it with my lips. Jockey's thumb plunged into my mouth. I had no time to wonder about what came over me. I slurped and sucked at my mate's thumb before giving the same treatment to his fingers, my tongue soaking each digit and nodding my head back and forth.

Jockey pulled his hand away. With his other hand he pinched the base of my dick, turning my shaft red in his lips. His eyes watched me as he reached down and shoved his spit-soaked hand under my ass, where he squeezed and groped a single cheek.

A wet thumb prodded at the rim of my asshole. Right as I cried out, Jockey began slurping his way down my cock again. His thumb popped inside of me.

Another surprise. I didn't recoil. Instead, the sensations were so overwhelming that I spread my thighs and sank as best I could to meet Jockey's thumb. I felt it wriggle its way into me. My dick throbbed harder inside his mouth. Still I pushed downward. I could feel his palm. His fingers groped me while that thumb circled inside of me.

I shot up. My hand found his left arm and I pulled. My cock popped free from his mouth as I was able to pull Jockey up.

"Oh, god," I gasped. "Why does that feel so fucking good? It shouldn't feel that good, should it?"

Jockey laughed between breaths. "You like that, huh?"

All I could do was nod. My cock bounced below my naval. I thought I could see a drop ready to glide out from my slit.

"Never had that done before, I take it?" Jockey said still grinning.

I shook my head. "God, no."

I jumped and moaned again when Jockey gave his thumb a wiggle before pulling it free from my ass.

A cunning smile played on his mouth, tilting one corner of his lips up, revealing dimples. He was leaning down towards me; his eyes took on a slanted quality and he grinned mischievously. The grin intrigued me; he was now my opponent as well as my comrade. I sensed this from my long familiarity with his expressions—Jockey was devising some kind of strategy. Soon it came out. He laughed, tweaked one of my nipples, and said, "If that's how good you feel with just my thumb imagine how much better my cock will feel."

"I don't know, man," I said, and my voice sounded weak and listless even to me.

"You'll be fine, baby. Trust me, you're in good hands." His voice was soothing, deep-throated, friendly, but somehow determined at the same time. He spoke to me as if it had already been agreed upon and he was merely giving directions now. "I've never been with anyone as beautiful as you... I wanna be inside you so bad it hurts."

Had I not just had my asshole licked out to the point I was in delirium then I may have laughed at how corny he was being. But instead, every one of those words felt true and packed with meaning. I was beautiful and if I gave him this part of myself it would be a special night for both of us.

"Whattaya say?"

I couldn't speak. Could barely think. So I just nodded.

Grabbing my thighs, he tugged me with no small amount of force toward him. His movements were calculated and powerful. With a single hand, he pressed back on one of my legs. I could feel my ass spreading.

He hawked a glob of spit over my hole and smeared it around with his fingers. Two more globs of spit found their way onto my asshole until I cold feel rivers of saliva dribbling down my crack.

Jockey watched me, blowing me little kisses as he rubbed his fingers around my entrance. I gasped when his tip began to slide up and down between my ass cheeks. It felt so much bigger than it had in my mouth. For several seconds, the wet tip simply glided between my buttocks. My thighs opened in response to the amazing sensation, beckoning Jockey's cock to take its rightful place.

Any fear I'd had about being fucked was slowly replaced with an eagerness to feel the erotic sensation of what was to come. If his cock felt anything like his thumb had then this was going to be fucking amazing. There was also the pesky virginity issue. I was impatient to ditch it. I was eighteen and keen to become a man—even if it meant allowing another man to do that for me. And so what if it was Jockey who I gave my cherry to. He was a close friend and maybe this would be something special for both of us. It was obvious he was really into me, and I suppose in the moment I was sort of into him too. Even if it was partly booze-fuelled.

The bulbous head settled onto the sensitive flesh of my asshole. Jockey pressed, and our flesh resisted one another. His cock mashed against me, but my asshole seemed to press back, refusing to give up its purity.

What happened next happened so fast. I felt a wet sensation, then more sliding. Suddenly, my skin spread around him. My asshole took shape tightly around Jockey's tip when it burst into me.

I had been breached.

It hurt. And it didn't. The soreness seemed to throb. The head of Jockey's prick was fattening inside my ass. I could feel the stiff strength positioned behind it. I could feel the man throbbing. The pain was nothing compared to any of this. The heat of Jockey's crotch enveloped me. It was all overwhelming.

Jockey hooked his arms around my legs, which now pointed toward the stars in the sky. I watched the moonlight highlight his features, which I was discovering were more handsome than I'd ever cared to admit. He seemed to move in closer. I felt this advance, because it pressed his dick further into me. My head fell back. My body widened around him inside. For all the soreness it continued to cause me, I was focused on the feeling of a dick burrowing deeper between my flesh. The slow and gradual taking of my innocence.

The pain was unlike anything I'd ever felt before and there was more than one moment where I considered asking him to pull out. But I soldiered on, determined to ride through to the pleasure he'd promised me. Eventually, though, my pain threshold was near breaking point and I had to ask, "Is it all the way in?"

"No," he said, "only about half."

Jockey must have sensed I was on the verge of asking him to pull out because he quickly rammed the remainder of his engorged cock straight up inside me, taking my breath away, bringing moisture to my eyes. The hard prick was buried to the very balls inside my unprepared body. "Now it's all in," he said with great satisfaction.

"Fucking hell, Jockey!" My fists punched the ground. "What the fuck did you do that for?"

"How else was I supposed to get it in?" His voice against my ear was strange, alarming in its newness, its roughness. There was something uncontrollable happening to Jockey now that he was embedded inside me. He was breathing very hard, and in a coarse, angry-sounding way which was, I knew, the result of his mounting lust, his eagerness to finish what he had begun.

"Seriously, bro," I hissed through clenched teeth. "I don't think you understand how fucking painful this is."

"Shut up," he said quietly, but seriously. "You can take it, Mikey, I know you can. It'll only hurt for a little while, then it will all be over. Just remember...it is my birthday."

"Fuck your birthday!"

"Fuck yourself," he murmured harshly, grinding himself so deeply inside me I felt him in my stomach. "Come on, bro... Don't be a fuckin' pussy about it. Hell, you let me dick you, you wanted it... now just lay there and take it like a man." I caught the subtle implications of contempt in his voice—contempt for having conquered me, for having found it so easy to trick me. And I had been tricked. Of that I was sure.

Stabbing in and out of my back passage, Jockey was taking ownership of body. He was a stranger in these wild moments, no longer aware that I was Michael, his good friend, no longer concerned with anything except the animal in himself which I, after all, had helped to elicit.

My groans of pain became louder, more urgent.

"Just hang on," he said, "you'll like it in a minute."

That minute lasted about five minutes. And then it was just as he said. I liked it. He thrust smoothly, carefully, never withdrawing very far before coming back to the hilt. I spread my legs wide and gripped his biceps, squeezing the vine-like tattoos inked into his skin, as he sawed in and out of my asshole, drilling me with increasing pleasure and excitement. The sensation of being filled, then emptied, then filled once more was incredible. I looked at him. Jockey's eyes were fixated on his cock, watching his length possess me again and again.

"I can't believe I'm fucking you," he said, smiling as he continued to watch his gliding shaft. "You definitely have the tightest hole I've ever rooted."

I lay there and watched his body work. His hard hairy stomach rolled. His arms and shoulders locked, his hands gripping my legs firmly and holding me in place. His expressions were what held most of my gaze, though. Tiny subtleties leapt out at me. His stubbled jaw would fall open with a slow gasp. His dark eyes would mist over and grow distant for the briefest seconds. The muscles in his neck would tighten and strain.

Soon I was gasping and moaning. Jockey enveloped me. His upper body seized, stiff and unyielding. His lower body rolled right through me. The rhythm was incredible. I wrapped my legs about his waist as best I could and held on. My need to wrap around him did not go unnoticed.

"You like this, don't cha?"

"Yeah. It feels good. *You* feel good."

"Told you so." He gave my upturned ass a light smack. "I knew you'd love being my bitch."

I didn't know how to respond to that so I gave him a mindless, "Yeah."

"Your Jockey's bitch aren't ya, Mikey?" He gave my ass another slap. "Can't get enough of Jockey's big dick."

"Yeah, man. Love your big dick."

"Fucking oath you do."

I don't know what possessed me to go along with his kinky talk. Whenever I'd heard similar stuff in porn I'd struggled not to laugh, but right now I was too caught up in the moment. And I knew the more I played along the more he'd give me those delicious fuck-punches that had my dick spurting precum all over my belly.

"Look at you," he said, slowing down as he sneered in contempt. "All strung out for my dick like a fag."

"Stop gloating and just fuck me you prick."

He laughed and did what I asked, fucking my ass so hard that each thrust of his hips forced his name past my lips. It became like a chant, a desperate moan I repeated again and again. *Jockey. Jockey. Jockey.* For too long my pretend soldier had been restricted to being my once-a-week cocksucker, little more than a convenient place to put my cock, but he was now showing me he had other talents, and a natural dominance I'd underestimated.

He leaned down and began kissing my neck and biting my chest, licking and sucking all around my nipples and collarbone. He was ravishing me like he couldn't get enough, all the while moving his cock in and out of me, claiming my cherry in his name.

"I'm close, Mikey." He grunted, pumping hard. "Where do you want it?"

I gave him my answer by hooking my legs around him tighter. I needed it. His essence, his love, his hate...whatever the fuck it was he'd been brewing in those big hairy balls of his.

A sharp pain dug into my stomach when Jockey's hips slammed into me in an attempt to bury his erection as far as he could. His jaw fell open. He made no sound. I felt how locked his entire body was. I knew it was happening. The final act that would forever connect us.

"Here it is," he whimpered. "Here. It. Fucking. Is."

I felt the warmth seep into me, watching in awe as he finally let forth a series of moans. His arm buckled. Jockey's sweat-soaked body collapsed on top of me. His chest pressed me into the ground with his every erratic breath. I could feel the base of his cock twitching in the ring of my asshole, unloading every drop of sperm he had.

My thighs ached from being spread wide. I ignored the feeling. Instead I focused on the dick that throbbed inside of me, filling me up with a scorching wetness. I gently whirled my hips, feeling how slick everything felt... even inside.

Jockey turned his face toward mine. For a while we just stared at one another gasping for air. I still wiggled beneath him, feeling his cock lose a bit of strength inside of me. When I couldn't resist anymore, I pressed my lips to his. I couldn't get enough of this feeling. Whatever it was, or why, I didn't care. It felt dirty and devious. I loved it.

When our lips finally parted, Jockey lifted himself on his hands and pulled away.

"Fucking hell," he said looking down at me. "That was amazing."

I smiled wearily. Jockey stared at me a few seconds longer, then I felt his hips drawing away from my body. His fleshy dick started to slither from my ass, leaving behind a reservoir of seed.

"Best birthday present ever," he chuckled and flopped down beside me.

For the longest time, all I could do was lay there staring at the night sky. Watching the moon watch us. I felt nasty and used, in the best way possible. The only question running through my head was *when can we do it again?*

The beginning...

A Note From Zane

THANK YOU SO MUCH FOR taking the time to read The First Time. Also, if you are keen to read more spicy tales similar to Broken Boys then I recommend checking out my Jock Shot series.

Thank you again for taking the time to read the opening chapter of Broken Boys. I really do appreciate your support and I hope you are keen to stay for the rest of Mike and Jockey's journey.

Zane

Also by Zane Menzy
CRASHING HEARTS

A SUMMER OF SEXUAL awakening like no other.

Keegan Andrews, a young man with a score to settle, is about to step into adulthood in reckless fashion by attempting to seduce his father's best friend, Damon Harris—an arrogant womanizer who has done Keegan wrong on the night of his eighteenth birthday.

What happens next takes both men by surprise. The unexpected heat and power of their passion unleashes a sexual awakening that threatens to expose long-kept secrets and send hearts crashing. And if they're not careful it might just change the very course of their lives...

CRASHING HEARTS is an edgy gay romance series packed with heat, heart and humour. It is a love story about the power of friendship, wild adolescence, and the importance of being true to one's self.

EDGE OF DECEIT

MILD-MANNERED ACCOUNTANT Dane Dravitski has always viewed his best mate Anton as a bright spark in his life, but unexpectedly that bright spark has ignited into a burning desire. Unfortunately, Anton is strictly a ladies' man, and Dane is forced to hide his heart's true feelings. However, a tantalising opportunity presents itself on a boys' night out, and Dane's burning desire begins to shed light on some very dark shadows.

Despite laidback appearances, Anton Matthews is a control freak who has known since a young age he was destined for success. A success that would help heal the scars of his troubled youth. Now at twenty-nine, and the danger of bankruptcy looming, he is growing impatient for some good fortune. To Anton's amazement a shocking revelation from Dane offers him a chance to rectify his situation but submitting to it will mean sacrificing his only protection; control.

As the raw love and painful history of their friendship is slowly revealed in a house haunted by its past and ghostly secrets, both men are forced to confront their demons while walking along the... *Edge of Deceit*.

LET ME CATCH YOU

DISCOVER "THE SECRET" in this haunting gay romance.

Fresh from university, Stephen Davis has returned to the family farm to inherit a responsibility that was never meant to be his. Feeling bored and trapped, the pretentious farm boy starts hanging out with Shaun Munro, an unpopular try-hard from the town's most dysfunctional family. What starts as an unlikely friendship slowly evolves into a passionate romance that takes Stephen completely by surprise. Sadly, their summer of love comes to a tragic end and Stephen's life is changed forever.

Twenty years later, Inver Murray has come home to Clifton to bury the father he barely knew. Despite his reluctance to be back in town, he does enjoy the chance to stay and reconnect with Stephen, his childhood neighbour. However, interactions with Stephen soon turn awkward, and strange happenings in the night begin to rattle Inver who is unaware that his handsome host intends to make him pay for the sins of his dead father.

Set along the wild coast of New Zealand, Let Me Catch You is a haunting love story that brings two broken souls together as they unearth the truth about what happened all those years ago when Shaun Munro learned "the secret."

About the Author

Zane lives in New Zealand in a rundown pink shack near the beach with his gaming-obsessed flatmate and a demanding cat. He is a fan of ghost stories, road trips, and nights out that usually lead to his head hanging in a bucket the next morning.

He enjoys creating characters who have flaws, crazy thoughts and a tendency to make bad decisions. His stories are steamy, unpredictable and tend to explore the darker edge of desire.

Milton Keynes UK
Ingram Content Group UK Ltd.
UKHW031913050224
437294UK00006B/315

9 798223 545439